Firestorm

by

Emerie A Knight

Long ago in a land far, far away, there lived a princess.

1. Princess

Sixteen-year-old Princess Elenore of Sundragon was definitely not what you might expect of a princess. Yes, her appearance was typical of a royal – lightly freckled, olive skin, piercing, ice-blue eyes, her striking, auburn hair part braided around her lower crown with the rest falling loose to the small of her back – yet she was anything but. She was never well-presented; if anything, she always looked like she had crawled through a hedge then rolled in mud. She wasn't graceful; far from it. She was the clumsiest person in the castle. She didn't care for etiquette, which frustrated her parents no end. In fact, there was only one word which could effectively describe Princess Elenore of Sundragon: wild and that's just how she liked it.

The kingdom of Sundragon, on the other hand, was *exactly* as you'd expect. It looked like something straight out of a story book. The outskirts were filled with stunning, glass-clear lakes, miles of well-tended farmland and sprawling, vivid green forests. The inner kingdom was home to charming, cobbled streets, picture perfect cottages and a colourful, central gardens which lay before the impressive, sand-coloured castle. The castle itself was surrounded by a high, stone wall and was adorned with gargoyles of dragons and ornate designs resembling suns. The castle belonged to the king and queen of Sundragon (Elenore's parents) and had been passed down through many generations. King Robert (Elenore's dad) was a kind and generous ruler and hoped that he could teach his daughter to be the same.

As the sun was beginning to set on a slow, summer evening, Elenore was out in the castle garden, playing with her pet hawk, Hank. She had rescued him two years ago as a fledgling when he had fallen out of a large oak tree and been abandoned by his parents. Since then, the two had become inseparable. Wherever the princess went, Hank went too. As you can imagine, having no human friends and only a hawk for company, Princess Elenore was still quite childish for a girl of sixteen and she had an incredible love of games. At that moment, Hank was flying *away* from Elenore as fast as his little wings could flap. Elenore charged up behind him and tapped him on the head. "Tag, Hank. You're it!" she giggled and ran away laughing. "Catch me if you can!" Poor Hank sighed and squawked in protest. *'Not again.'* he thought. Nonetheless, he changed direction and began to chase after his human for what felt like the thousandth time that day.

Whilst she was running, Elenore started to daydream. She always daydreamed when she was playing in the garden. She would imagine she was in one of the forests she could see from her bedroom window, running free and looking for adventure. Her parents had never let her leave the castle walls. They said it was for her own safety until she turned eighteen. This she understood but it still felt unfair to keep her away from the rest of the world when all she longed for was to be a part of it. *'What would it be like,'* she wondered, *'to weave in and out of the trees, to meet new people, to make friends or to have an adventure?'* All those things seemed so far away and her parents seemed more bothered with getting her to behave like a 'proper' princess so that they could marry her off than allowing her to fulfil her dreams.
'That's another thing,' she thought to herself, *'I don't want to get married!'.* Elenore couldn't begin to think why she should want to attach herself to some boring royal for the rest of her life. In fact, she could think of nothing worse than having to sit through boring meetings, dull dinners and even more bland conversation with whomever it was that her parents decided was worthy. No doubt they would choose someone

with a large kingdom and lots of money. Elenore couldn't imagine that her parents would allow her to marry for anything other than the good of the kingdom, though she knew they themselves were, actually, very much in love.

Suddenly, the princess was dragged aggressively out of her daydream by the high-pitched shouts of her childhood nanny, Sally. "Princess Elenore, his majesty requests your presence at the dining table *immediately!*" She barked. Elenore came to an abrupt stop and pivoted on her heel. She sped past Hank, knocking him sideways, and skidded to stand in front of the nanny.
"Was that quick enough for you, Sally?" she asked with a grin. Sally looked Elenore over disapprovingly, wrinkling her nose in disgust.
"And might I suggest you clean yourself up quickly before you make an appearance!" Sally scoffed. With that, Nanny Sally stalked off, brushing her pinafore and muttering to herself about the state of the princess as she went. She left the castle door open, indicating that Elenore should follow her.
"Does she *ever* smile?" Elenore mused. "She needs to lighten up, right Hank...Hank?" Realising that Hank was not beside her, Elenore turned around to see where he was hiding. She finally noticed him perched tentatively on a bird bath, looking disgruntled and disorientated from being knocked over. "Oh, Hank, I'm sorry! I didn't realise I knocked you that hard. I was just in such a rush..."

Her apology was interrupted by Nanny Sally calling from inside, "Princess Elenore, his highness is waiting!" Sally was sounding grouchier by the second. Elenore looked at Hank and they both sighed, exchanging a knowing look.
"She sounds *really* cross, Hank. I guess we'd better hurry before she turns red in the face and steam starts puffing out of her ears!" Elenore smirked. Hank chirped in agreement

and the pair hastily scurried through the enormous castle doors and entrance hallway down to the arched oak door to the dining room. "No time to clean up, Hank, Sally said they're waiting now," Elenore whispered, brushing the front of her dress with grubby hands before she pushed with all her weight on the left door and it slowly creaked open. Breathless from the effort, the princess muttered to herself, "We just *had* to have the fancy, heavy doors, didn't we? Honestly, people are so inconsiderate..."

"Ahem."

Elenore looked up sharply and stopped muttering as she heard a cough from across the room. Her father (King Robert) was sat at the head of a long, elegant dining table. His piercing blue eyes were staring straight at Elenore and his eyebrows were arched expectantly as he waited for her to speak.

"Sorry I'm late Papa, I mean *father*. Hank and I were just playing outside and..." Elenore trailed off as she became increasingly aware of how messy she was. Her hands, dress and feet were covered in muddy marks (she never wore shoes in the garden and, in her rush, had forgotten to put any on for dinner) and her hair was wild and windswept with her braids loose and unkempt. She fiddled with the bundle of hair which fell over her shoulder and looked pleadingly at her father.

King Robert sighed with great effort and brushed his hand across his neatly kept, deep brown beard. With his piercing blue eyes (like his daughters) he glanced across at his wife – Elenore's mother and queen of Sundragon – who sat next to him. She was watching Elenore with a small smile flickering on her oval face and a glint of affection in her soft, emerald eyes. Her hair was auburn, like her daughter's but, unlike Elenore's, it was braided neatly and tightly beneath her crown with no loose hair. "Elenore, what have I told you about cleaning yourself up before dinner?" Robert asked.

"I know father but Sally said..."

"It doesn't matter what Sally said, Elenore. You are a *princess* and you need to start acting like one!" Robert didn't often raise his voice, but he had sharpened his tone and was visibly annoyed. Elenore was frozen to the spot, still holding the door handle. Her eyes started to glisten with the beginnings of tears which were threatening to form.

"I'm sorry Papa, I didn't think I..."

"Well perhaps you *should* think, for goodness sake!" Robert snapped. The princess let her arm drop from the door and lowered her eyes, ashamed. The queen – Lydia – placed her hand on the king's elbow.

"Oh Robert," she soothed, "leave the child be. She's been playing and ran out of time. Let's eat, dear?" King Robert looked at his wife, over to his daughter, back to his wife and let out a heavy breath in defeat.

"Alright Lydia, as you wish. Sit down, Elenore, let's have dinner. But next time, *please* clean up first." Robert gestured to a chair which was pulled out from the table ready. Elenore padded softly over to the chair, close to where her father was sitting. She hovered just behind it, unsure of whether to sit down as she didn't want to be told off anymore. She looked at the king, trying to decide what to do. King Robert noticed Elenore's unsettled expression and his own face softened into a smile. "Come and sit down, you big dummy! I'm sorry for being mean. Do you think you can forgive your grumpy old Papa?" The princess plonked herself down on the chair and grinned.

"Only if you stop calling me *Elenorc*."

"Oh, alright then, my little Nell. Let's eat!"

2. Nell

When Princess Elenore was small, perhaps four years old, she made friends with the only other child in the castle. He was Nanny Sally's son and was just a year older than Elenore herself. He was always there whenever Sally was caring for the princess and so the two got to know one another. The first day they were introduced, Elenore couldn't pronounce her friend's name. His name was Christopher but the young princess began calling him Kiffy. Christopher giggled and accepted the name as his own. They quickly became best friends and spent much of their time together. Kiffy and Princess Elenore were well known to the castle staff for their mischievous antics and boisterous play. They were extremely hard to keep up with and, as one was part of the royal family and the other lived in the servants' quarters, no area of the castle was safe. Kiffy helped Elenore explore the kitchens, living quarters and laundries of his home. In return, Elenore showed Kiffy the cavernous rooms and corridors in which she lived. The king and queen were overjoyed by the friendship and allowed them to roam wherever they pleased. The servants, on the other hand, simply couldn't wait get rid of them.

Each day, the princess and her best friend seemed to be causing havoc somewhere in the castle. They fed the horses and let them out of the stables; they tangled themselves up in freshly laundered bedding and ran around the gardens pretending to be ghosts. One afternoon, they even changed the salt and sugar round in the kitchens meaning that all the meals were unusually sweet that evening. Somehow, they still mostly managed to avoid a scolding from Nanny Sally and the other servants. Many of them even became quite fond of the disastrous duo and looked forward to the next chaotic event.

Once the princess turned six, Kiffy was shortened to Kiff and Elenore craved a nickname of her own. It was the one thing she asked Kiff for on her birthday. Kiff would not oblige because, now seven, it wasn't cool for him to think of a nickname for her. It wasn't even that cool to be friends with a girl, but there were no other children in the castle and she was his *best* friend. Princess Elenore didn't like how long her name was; she always felt like she was being told off when she heard it. She sulked for a week after her birthday came and went with no nickname, but eventually forgot about it until one summer's evening in the gardens.

The children had built their own wooden house in one of the large oak trees in the castle garden – with a little help from Nanny Sally. They were sat in their treehouse planning their next move. "I think we should try the stables again." Kiff suggested, brushing his sand coloured hair out of his warm, hazel eyes and scrunching up his nose in thought.
"We could, but what would we do there?" Elenore asked, unsure.
"Well, maybe we could go for a ride. You have your own horse, right? And I'm sure there's a spare one for me."
"You're right!" Elenore exclaimed, jumping up from the small log seat, "That's a fantastic idea! Come on, let's go and check out the stables now so we can work out the details." As she ran to the treehouse doorway, Elenore tripped and went flying through the gap headfirst. Kiff saw her fall and lunged after her, reaching his arms out to grab her. "Nell!" He yelled, in such a panic that he couldn't get his words out properly. The seven-year-old managed to grab the princess' ankle to prevent her from falling but he was still only young and couldn't hold on for long.

Meanwhile, hanging upside-down, Princess Elenore was swinging her arms wildly, trying to grab onto a nearby branch. She started to wiggle her body to get closer to the branch. "What're you doing?" Kiff yelled down from the treehouse. "I can't hold on for much longer!"

"I need to get to that branch!" Elenore shouted back and carried on swinging. As she made a fourth attempt to grab the branch, Kiff lost his grip on her ankle and she went plummeting down towards the ground.

"NO!" Kiff cried as he watched her drop. He started to sob as she crumpled on the floor "N... El..." After a moment's pause, Kiff slid down the treehouse ladder and ran to Elenore's side, tears streaming down his face. "H...Help!" He bawled, unable to speak properly through the sobs.

Nanny Sally, who was in the laundry room talking to one of the maids at the time, heard Kiff's cries for help and ran down to the treehouse to see what was wrong. She was met with a very dramatic sight. "Christopher!" She shouted, "What happened?" on hearing Sally's voice, Elenore lifted her head and looked round.

"Ouch!" she moaned, "My leg *really* hurts."

"El... but... I thought... no... you're okay?" stuttered Kiff.

"I'm fine, you dummy," teased Elenore, "except for this stupid leg. Nanny Sally, can you help me up please?" As Sally lifted Elenore, with her hands under the little girl's armpits, onto her feet, Kiff wiped the tears from his face. Elenore winced as she tried to put weight on her right leg. "Ouch!"

"Be careful, Princess Elenore," warned Sally with a caring undertone to her stern voice. "Here, come and sit on the bench so I can check your leg." Elenore started to limp over to a small wooden bench by the garden path when Kiff quickly caught up with her and allowed her to lean on him to help. "Anyway, I think you just came up with my nickname, Kiff." The princess said with a small smile.

"What do you mean?" Kiff asked as they sat down, puzzled.

"What you shouted when I fell – Nell." She replied.

"Oh, but I just got my letters all muddled." Kiff admitted, blushing.

"Well I like it." Elenore replied, "From now on, I'd like to be called Nell."

Kiff looked at Nell with a lopsided grin and brushed his hair out of his eyes. "Nell," he said as if considering it carefully, "I think it suits you."

"Well you'll have to broach the subject with the king and queen first as I'm not sure they would approve of other people calling you 'Nell', Princess Elenore," interrupted Sally. "I for one certainly shan't be calling you anything but your full title." Nell looked at the floor, trying to hold back a giggle. Abruptly, the nanny yanked her foot hard.

"Ah!" she cried.

"There," Sally muttered, "that's better."

"What was *that* for?" winced Nell.

"It was a simple dislocation, princess. I've simply relocated your ankle." Sally explained, triumphant.

"Well it *hurt*." Nell protested.

"Stand up and try to walk on it now," Sally gestured with her hands for the princess to stand. Nell looked at her doubtfully.

"Well, go on then," Sally prompted.

Slowly, Nell pushed herself up from the bench and tentatively put some of her weight on her damaged leg. Her eyes widened in surprise. "That's... a lot better! Thank you, Nanny Sally!"

Sally replied with a satisfied smile, "I thought it would be. Now, Princess Elenore, you must go and speak to your parents at once and let them know what happened. Christopher, I'll speak to *you* about this shortly." She glared at Kiff, who was still sat on the bench, and he shuffled uncomfortably.

"Sally, none of this was Kiff's fault," Nell explained, "I fell out of the treehouse and he tried to save me."

"That's very kind of you, princess, but Christopher and I will still need to have words." The caring tone in Sally's voice had been replaced with a hint of exasperation and Kiff knew he would be getting told off once Nell had gone.

"Okay but please be kind to him," pleaded Nell.

"I'll take your request into consideration, Princess Elenore," Sally nodded officially, "now hurry along to your parents. They are currently in the drawing room taking afternoon tea."

"Yes, Nanny Sally, right away," Nell bobbed her head in a small, polite curtsey and walked quickly towards the front doors, still with a slight limp.

Nell hobbled into the drawing room to find her parents reading quietly. They both looked up, surprised, as she entered the room. "Elenore, are you alright?" asked Queen Lydia (her mother), "You look unhappy."

King Robert looked towards her feet, "And your ankle is swollen! What *have* you been doing child?" Her father looked back up at her face, his eyebrows furrowed with concern.

"It's okay, Papa, I just fell out of the treehouse," Nell whispered.

"You did *what?*" the queen asked, horrified.

"Mama, I just tripped over and fell through the door," Nell tried to explain, "I was rushing to get out and fell but Kiff caught me and..."

"Kiff?" King Robert demanded, "Is *he* why you fell out of the tree?"

"No, Papa!" Nell cried, "he tried to *stop* me from falling. I tripped as I was leaving the treehouse and fell through the door but Kiff; Kiff grabbed hold of my ankle as I fell. He would've managed to stop me from falling completely if I hadn't been a dummy and tried to grab onto a branch." The princess looked at both her parents imploringly. "It wasn't his fault."

King Robert took a deep breath and calmed himself down before replying, "Right, so Kiff was trying to help?"

"Yes!" Nell replied, "But when I fell, I dislocated my ankle so Nanny Sally relocated it and told me to come and tell you what happened."

"Robert," Queen Lydia whispered tensely to her husband, "don't say anything irrational."

"Papa?" Nell prompted, trying to read his expression.

King Robert sighed and got up to crouch beside his daughter. "My darling little one, is your ankle feeling better since Nanny Sally relocated it?" he asked.

"Yes, Papa."

"And Kiff is *not* the reason you fell out of the treehouse?"

"No, Papa, he tried to save me." King Robert looked his child in the eyes, searching them for any hint of deception. When he found none, satisfied, he turned to his wife.

"Lydia, we must make sure the children are supervised during play from now on, do you agree?"

"Of course I do, my love. I couldn't bear it if something like that were to happen again." Nell's mother replied

"Would you then have a word with Nanny Sally to make sure she supervises them properly?" King Robert asked.

"Yes, I will go at once."

"Mama," Nell interjected.

"Yes, my child?"

"Before you go, there's something else. Kiff *finally* thought of a nickname for me, even if it was sort of by accident."

King Robert, looking amused, asked, "Oh, what is it, Elenore?" He knew how desperately the princess had wanted to be given a nickname.

"Nell," replied the princess in a matter-of-fact tone. "I like it and I'd like it if you'd accept it too, if that's alright." Both of Nell's parents looked at her in silence for a few moments, contemplating her request and processing the name.

King Robert was the one to speak first, "Did you know that Nell means bright, shining one? I'd say that describes you well."

"It *is* rather lovely, isn't it, Robert?" Queen Lydia added.

"I think that's a wonderful idea, little one. We can call you Nell if that is what you would prefer." The king nodded.

"Oh, thank you Papa!" the young princess cried and threw her arms around her father. "That *is* what I'd prefer. Thank you!"

During the following winter, Kiff's father came to the castle. He needed to take his son home to start to shadow his work and learn his trade as a blacksmith. This meant he could no longer stay in the castle. Kiff and Nell both took the news hard. They cried as they shared an emotional goodbye and Nell refused to leave her bedroom for a month. They wrote to each other every week for three and a half years until Nell was eleven and Kiff was twelve. That year, Nell's weekly letters never received a reply. She carried on writing for three months until she gave up hope. The princess was heartbroken but her mother and father convinced her that it was for the best and she could now concentrate fully on her studies.

Although she never mentioned Kiff to her family again, she still chose to keep her nickname. By the week of her twelfth birthday, even the stable hands knew her as Princess Nell. In fact, the only person who refused to call her anything but Princess Elenore was Nanny Sally, Kiff's mother. Although her son had returned home, Nanny Sally remained at the castle to care for and tutor the princess as she grew. After her best friend had deserted her, Nell began to harbour a deep dislike for her nanny. Sally reminded her of the times she wanted to bury at the back of her brain and forget. She missed him.

3. Dragons

Princess Nell and her parents had just finished their dinner after their earlier argument. Hank was perched on a high stool next to Nell's chair. "So, what have you done this afternoon, Nell – apart from coating yourself in mud in the gardens?" her mother, Queen Lydia, asked.

"Well I..." Nell was interrupted suddenly by an urgent knock at the door. The king and queen exchanged a worried glance and looked back at the door. The knock came a second time, slightly louder and more insistent than the first. King Robert sighed and stood up reluctantly.

"This had better be good," he muttered to himself.

As he walked towards the door, the insistent knocker ran out of patience and opened the door themselves. Nanny Sally stood in the doorway looking shocked.

"I'm so sorry to interrupt, your majesties, but... you see..." Sally paused as though unsure how to voice what she needed to say.

"What's the matter, Sally?" asked Queen Lydia, tentatively.

"I didn't know what to do, your majesty, so I came straight to you," she wavered.

"Nanny Sally, what *is* it?" asked Nell impatiently.

"Dragons," Sally breathed.

"What?" exclaimed King Robert.

"There are dragons in the skies outside the castle," Sally looked visibly shaken as she finished her sentence. King Robert rushed out of the dining room door, through the hallway and flung open the gigantic castle doors. He stared up into the sky, his eyes full of fear. They widened further still when he saw the scene Sally described for himself.

"Dragons," he murmured, clasping one hand to his jaw in disbelief.

The queen and princess hurried to King Robert's side to see if what Sally had said was true. Queen Lydia gripped her husband's shoulder and held Nell's hand to keep her in the great doorway of the castle. She peered out of the opening and was struck by the same fear as the king. "Robert?" she muttered, "There... there are dragons." She tightened her grasp on both King Robert's shoulder and the princess' hand as though she needed their support to stay standing.

Nell was desperate to run outside and see the dragons for herself but her mother held her hand tightly so that she could barely see out of the door. She strained her neck and titled her head upwards to try and get a better view of the creatures in the sky outside. "Mama, let go, I can't see!" she complained, but her mother only tightened her grip. From where she was standing, she could make out large, winged silhouettes against the blaze of the setting sun. They looked a little like oversized birds but with pointed wings. The princess was desperate to get closer; she had never seen a dragon before and her heart was fit to burst with excitement.

After gathering his composure, King Robert took both his wife and daughter by the hand with a new-found conviction and took them back into the dining room by marching quickly but calmly. "Sally," Robert called to the nanny.

"Yes, your majesty?" Sally replied, peering round the dining room door and trying to keep herself from panicking.

"I'd like you to send for Lawrence immediately – I need to discuss the matter with him so that it can be sorted in a timely manner," the king ordered.

"Of course, immediately, your majesty," Sally chirped and bustled hastily out of the dining room to send for Lawrence, the captain of the guard.

Once the family were alone, Queen Lydia rushed to her husband's side. "What are we going to do, Robert? There haven't been reports of dragons in Sundragon since...

since... well, for hundreds of years! Why have they left the mountains?"

"I'm not sure, my love. I'm as surprised as you are about this. The dragons haven't been in this kingdom since long before my time," King Robert replied.

Nell looked at her parents, unable to believe the words she was hearing, "Wait, what? You mean to say that you *knew* there were dragons living in the mountains? *Dragons?* And you didn't think that this was something that I needed to know? You've always said that dragons are the stuff of fairy tales, Papa, but now you're telling me they're real!"

"No, Nell, we thought it better not to tell you and I believe I made the right choice not to! Dragons are to be feared *not* admired!" King Robert replied emphatically.

"But why do we fear them? Legend says they used to *live* in the kingdom! So, they can't be that scary. I assume, since they are real, the legends are probably true as well." Nell argued.

"Now is *not* the time to be discussing silly, childhood legends, Elenore," Queen Lydia snapped. Upon hearing her full name, the princess became quiet whilst her parents continued to discuss the issue at hand in ever more panicked tones.

Throughout this conversation, Hank was still perched on his stool at the table hopping from foot to foot wondering what on earth was going on. The noise and raised voices were startling and he could sense the tension and rising panic in the room. He let out a loud squawk which caused the family to fall silent and turn to look in his direction. Once their attention was focused on him, he flapped his wings forcefully then glided to land on Nell's shoulder. "Oh Hank, I'm sorry," she cooed, "It's all getting a little loud in here isn't it?" Hank ruffled his feathers in agreement. "You see, there are *dragons* in the skies outside!" Hank's eyes grew wide as he heard the word. Hank had listened to Nell explain the many legends of Sundragon to him more than once. She had a large book with lots of pictures and he remembered the picture of the dragon vividly. Hank shuddered as he thought about it and nestled into Nell's tangled hair by her neck. "Don't worry, Hank," the princess whispered comfortingly, "they can't see us in here." Unconvinced, Hank remained nuzzled into the wild bundles of hair on the princess' shoulder.

At that moment, the captain of the guard burst in through the dining room doors. "Your majesty, I got here as quickly as I could!" he said, his breathing heavy as though he had been running. Lawrence made his way over to where the king was sitting and leant on the table, exasperated. "What do you think we should do about the situation?"
King Robert rubbed his palm across his beard whilst attempting to think. "We should ensure the people of the kingdom remain inside until the dragons have returned to the mountains," the king decided. "Once the dragons have gone, we can try to understand what may have cause them to fly over the kingdom."
"A brilliant plan, your majesty," Lawrence agreed, "I will rally my men so that we can inform the people at once."
"Thank you, Lawrence," said the king, gratefully.
At once, the captain of the guard strode quickly to the doors of the dining room and through to the hallway. King Robert and Queen Lydia got up and followed him to see him out of the castle.

Nell decided to follow, with Hank still on her shoulder, just in case she could sneak another look at the dragons outside. Lawrence stopped at the castle doors and waited for the royals to reach him. As they reached the captain, there was a large roar from outside. A startled Hank flew off Nell's shoulder and into the gardens. "Hank!" cried the princess, lunging through the castle doors after her pet bird before anyone else could react. She sprinted into the middle of the gardens to the bird bath on which Hank had settled. "Come on Hank, you can't be out here," she whispered to him. As she picked him up and held him to her chest, Princess Nell happened to look up to the sky. She stood in awe staring at the magnificent creatures circling the castle. They were so powerful yet graceful in their movements and they were every bit as formidable as she had imagined as a child. She could see all the fantastic colours of the different dragons, deep blues, vivid greens, flame oranges and midnight blacks. She was mesmerised.

The king and queen looked through the castle entrance in a state of panic. They were calling out to Nell fearfully. "Elenore! Come back here at once!" cried Queen Lydia.
"Nell, Nell please hurry! You can't be out there!" shouted her father.
Lydia muttered to her husband, "Robert, we have to *do* something."
"Yes, you're right!" the king replied and immediately raced to where Nell was standing, still gazing up at the sky. Before he could reach her, an enormous, blood red dragon swooped down from the clouds and scooped up both Nell and Hank in one claw. The dragon shrieked menacingly at the king and took off again into the heavens. King Robert watched helplessly as his daughter was carried away across the horizon in the grip of a ferocious dragon. As he tracked the dragon through the sky, he thought he noticed a figure silhouetted against the sun (now almost set) on the dragon's back. He blinked, trying to focus on the figure more clearly but as suddenly as the silhouette appeared, it seemed to vanish. All the other dragons started to follow the kidnapper back towards the mountains.

King Robert turned back to the castle to see his wife looking broken and kneeling on the floor with her head in her hands.

He looked at Lawrence, who bowed his head in sympathy for the great loss the king and queen had just suffered. Queen Lydia began to sob loudly. The king rushed back to the doors, sweeping Lydia into an embrace to comfort her. "Why, Robert," the queen whispered through the tears, "why our baby?"

"I don't know, my love," her husband soothed.

"We have to *do* something!" she insisted.

"There is nothing we *can* do," sighed Robert, hopelessly.

"Can you at least send out a search party?" the queen continued.

Lawrence responded, "Yes, your majesties. My men and I will head out at once. Perhaps we will find her." The king and queen lingered in the castle entrance as the captain of the guard mounted his horse and galloped away to start the search. For now, all they could do was wait.

*

Through the claws of the dragon, Nell could see the forests speeding past in a swirl of green. Hank was still pressed to her chest, too afraid to move. She looked up at the dragon and started to shout, "Hey, you big bully. Let me go!" Hank squeaked in fear. "Oh Hank," Nell whispered, "we'll be alright, you'll see." The princess started to twist, turn and wriggle and the dragon's grip began to loosen. "Look, Hank, we're nearly out of its... w... woah!" The dragon's claw had opened just enough that Nell and Hank had fallen through the gap and plummeted towards the forest below. The dragon didn't appear to notice that its hostages had escaped and continued to fly overhead. Luckily, there were many layers of leaves in the forest which softened the princess' fall. She wasn't too seriously injured but as she hit the ground, everything went black.

4. Lost

Feeling a little groggy, Princess Nell slowly opened her eyes to find herself sprawled across a large bramble bush. Hank was laying on her chest with his wings spread wide and his head to one side. She could hear him breathing quietly. "OUCH!" she yelped as the sharp thorns of the brambles dug into her body when she tried to move. This roused Hank from his slumber and he flapped, startled, up to the branch of the nearest tree. He squawked grumpily at Nell. "Oh, calm down, Hank. I'm just trying to get off this... this... what is this thing anyway?" Wincing from the sharp pricks like needles in her skin, the princess slid as gently as she could off the bush, stood up and collapsed on the floor. "Ahh!" she cried after trying to put weight on her left foot. As she sat on the grass, Nell cradled her ankle which was swollen and red. "I must've hurt it somehow," she pondered as she looked around her. "How *did* we get here Hank?" she asked, rubbing the back of her head, as she took in the grassy floor, bushy undergrowth and looming, skyscraper trees touching the glow of the morning sun in her surroundings. All memory of what had happened at the castle the evening before had vanished when she hit her head on her descent from the dragon's claw. Hank looked at Nell, bemused. He couldn't remember either.

*

Meanwhile, on the outskirts of the same forest, Prince James was out hunting with his trusty steed called Firestorm. However, Firestorm was not a horse. He was a dragon, a magnificent creature of golden yellow with a strong, muscular body and glistening spiny wings. Firestorm was only a teenager and not yet fully grown so he was only around the size of a large stallion and he *loved* hunting with the prince. That morning, they were on the hunt for wild boar and Firestorm had picked up the scent of a large one further into the foliage. He charged forwards, gliding skillfully between the trees with James on his back. "Come on now, Firestorm, surely you can fly faster than that! Or are you getting tired in your old age?" James laughed. The dragon snorted and readily accepted the challenge. With a forceful flap of his wings, he propelled himself and the prince forwards at alarming speed, all the while keeping focused on the boar ahead of him. Firestorm glanced up at James and let out a triumphant puff as they began to advance on their prey. "That's more like it, Firestorm," James exclaimed gleefully, "look at us go!"

The pair sped through the forest, getting ever closer to the boar. Suddenly, Prince James brought his dragon to an abrupt stop. "Woah, Firestorm!" he shouted. Firestorm thumped to the ground and reared onto his hind legs in protest, exceedingly disgruntled to be stopped when he was nearly touching his prey. He turned around to stare at James and roared at him as if to say, '*What do you think you're doing?*' But the prince was distracted and gazing searchingly through the undergrowth. Firestorm followed his eyes and began looking for whatever his rider had seen and found nothing. He was about to roar again when he heard an enchanting, sweet melody soaring over the trees. It was a human singing. A *girl*. He couldn't believe it; Prince James had stopped their hunt for a *girl*. Firestorm blew billows of smoke from his nostrils in disgust.

"Listen! You hear that, Firestorm?" James whispered, coughing slightly from the smoke. The dragon growled quietly, unable to understand why Prince James would need to stop their hunt for a silly song. "Sounds pretty good right?" James continued. Firestorm growled louder this time and threw James off his back in annoyance. The dragon thought this would get a reaction out of him but instead, James simply picked himself back up and walked, entranced, towards the sound. Firestorm shook his head in disbelief, stunned that his friend would ignore him. "Hey, Firestorm," James called back arrogantly. The irritated dragon snapped his head to look at the prince. "Reckon I can rush in, save the fair maiden and have her swooning in my arms before the sun is fully risen?" wagered James. Firestorm glanced at the sky and saw that the sun was nearly fully above the horizon. He blew a small puff of smoke from his nostrils, making it a challenge. "I'll do it, you'll see!" James winked, and ran through the overgrown bushes in the direction from which he could hear the voice.

*

Nell was sitting on the ground of the clearing, still cradling her ankle and humming to herself to calm her nerves. The swelling had gone down a little, but it was still extremely tender. Hank hovered nearby, fluttering back and forwards with a look of worry and panic spreading across his face as he realised that they were both lost with no idea how they got to this place and no idea how to get home. They both stopped, frozen, when they heard a loud rustling coming from the undergrowth on the outside of the clearing. Hank zoomed to Nell's shoulder and hid behind the knotted mess of hair which fell near her neck. The princess began to back away slowly, unsure and uneasy. "Hank, nobody mentioned there might be *animals* out here. What if it's a bear?" Nell started to panic. Hank squawked. "You're right," she agreed, "what if it's a *tiger* or a *lion* or... wait, do they have those in forests?" Princess Nell was interrupted as the rustling got even noisier and then a tall figure came crashing through the bushes. "Ah!" Nell screamed as she ran backwards as fast as her damaged ankle would take her.

With a swish of his cape and a flick of his ruffled, sandy blonde hair, Prince James announced, "Fear not, fair maiden, for I am here to rescue you from... from..." as the prince looked around, he realised there was no imminent danger, "well, what *do* you need rescuing from exactly?" Nell stood up straight and looked at James properly now that the panic she felt had dissipated. She was a little bemused as the thing that had appeared was not a bear nor was it a tiger or lion. It was simply a human. Then she realised that the person had asked her a question and was waiting for an answer.
"Rescuing? I think you've got the wrong clearing..." Nell started.
"But... of course you need saving! I heard you singing in the forest; I cannot leave a damsel in distress." James said emphatically. Nell looked James up and down, even more perplexed but a little amused. She couldn't help but think she recognised him from somewhere; the sandy hair, the warm hazel eyes and his bravado seemed extremely familiar.

No matter how she tried to place him, the princess couldn't quite manage it. She shook her head in annoyance and returned her focus to the situation at hand. "I'm very sorry, but I think you have mistaken me for someone else. I'm not a damsel, I'm not in distress and I *certainly* don't need saving," she retorted. James paused for a moment. It was his turn to look puzzled. He looked long and hard at Nell, unsure of how to judge her. She certainly looked in distress; her auburn hair was knotted and wild with little twigs sticking out at various points, her dress was torn and muddied and her ankle looked injured. He was sure that she needed help but why would she not admit it? He glanced at her ice blue eyes and was hit by a jolt of recognition. He knew her from somewhere. But where?

"Oh, are you sure you don't? Only, you look a little lost and hurt," James replied slowly, gesturing to Nell's swollen ankle.

"No, I'm quite alright thank you," Nell insisted, hiding her ankle behind her other foot, "Hank and I are just on our way home."

"So... you're not in trouble?" James double checked.

"No, not in trouble."

"And you don't need saving, at all?"

"Nope," Nell confirmed, getting a little agitated.

"Not even a little bit?" the prince tried.

"I'm afraid not," Nell replied bluntly. She'd had enough and began to walk – although it was more of a hobble – past Prince James to sit on a nearby tree stump.

Hank chose this moment to peek out of Nell's hair and began squawking unhappily. He glanced over at the prince, focused back on Nell and continued his incessant chirping. "Oh, don't worry Hank," Nell soothed, "this gentleman was just leaving."

"I was? Hang on miss... miss... sorry what was your name?" James asked, confused.

The princess paused, unsure how much she should reveal to a complete stranger. She didn't know who he was or what his intentions really were; perhaps it would be best if he didn't know her true identity. She would use her middle name.

"Fleur," the princess muttered.

"Pardon?"

"Fleur. *Princess* Fleur." Nell exaggerated her annunciation since she felt that clearly this person was unable to understand her.

Prince James, again noted the state of her torn dress, her mud smudged cheeks and the tangled bird's nest of hair trailing down her back. "A princess," he whispered under his breath, "well I didn't see that one coming."

"And who, exactly, are you; storming into my clearing like you own the place?" demanded Nell. James' face fell as he realised that she had no idea who he was.

"I am *Prince* James of Skyrain," James said indignantly.

"Who?" mused Nell.

"This is my kingdom so yes, I *do* own the place," continued James, ignoring Nell's clear taunt. "and I think you'll find you're trespassing! I was hunting wild boar with my dragon, Firestorm, this morning and I heard your voice. I was simply trying to help..."

Nell interrupted him, her eyes widening, "You have a dragon?" This threw the prince of guard as it was the first time the princess had been almost approachable.

As he was gathering his thoughts, Hank pecked Nell on the ear. "Ouch, Hank!" yelped Nell, "what was that for?" Hank squawked pointedly at James, intimating that they should leave whilst he was distracted. "Yes, I agree Hank, but he has a *dragon*. I have to see it," whispered Nell. Hank let out an exasperated sigh and settled on the princess' shoulder looking extremely unimpressed. Princess Nell turned back round as she heard the prince begin to speak again.

"Yes, *princess*, I have a dragon. He should be right..." James trailed off as he turned around to find Firestorm had wandered off in his boredom.

"I don't see him, are you sure he's not imaginary?" Nell smirked.

"No, he's definitely real," replied James irately, "FIRESTORM, get back here!"

Firestorm was flying overhead, circling the clearing in which Nell and James were standing. He still couldn't believe that Prince James, his best friend, would ditch him and their hunt for some stupid *girl*. He snorted smoke out of his powerful nostrils; smoke so hot it threatened to combust. When the dragon heard James' shouts, he thought that the prince must've come to his senses after all. They would be able to get back to their hunt. Excitedly, Firestorm shot through the humongous trees like an arrow to where James was standing. He landed less than gracefully, knocking James sideways in the process. The wind, which his wings created as they closed, propelled Hank off Nell's shoulder and into a hole in the trunk of a large pine tree. Nell stood there astounded, her mouth hanging open and unable to fathom any words. Firestorm, though initially less than impressed that the human who halted his hunt was still there, soon began to grow curious. He padded over to her with his huge, clawed feet and began to sniff her hair as if he were a dog. Nell giggled excitedly.

"Don't worry, he's friendly," reassured James, although the princess was practically levitating with happiness. The dragon carried on sniffing Nell's face and clothes, treading a careful circle around her. After his second circle, Firestorm pushed the princess sideways with his forehead and snorted appreciatively. "Huh, I guess he likes you, princess," James mumbled.

"He says yes, I smell comforting. Though, he wants me to tell you that his name isn't Firestorm, it's Chuck," Nell replied.

"Chuck?" exclaimed James.

"Yes, he thinks Firestorm is way over the top," she smirked.

"You cannot be serious," James muttered, unimpressed, "and you know this how, exactly, Princess Fleur?" Nell started at the sound of her middle name; she had better get used to it if the prince was sticking around!

"He told me," Nell stated confidently.

"Oh yeah, sure, because *you* can speak dragon," James responded, his voice dripping with sarcasm.

Nell paused for a moment as she thought about it properly before whispering, almost inaudibly, "I guess I can."

Nell stood, stunned, at the realisation only to be distracted by *Chuck* the dragon as he nuzzled the palm of her hand as it hung by her side. Hank hovered behind the princess with his chest puffed out and his feathers fluffed, incredibly unhappy – and a little jealous. Hank let out a miffed squawk which startled Nell and she turned around to speak to him. "Yes, you're right Hank. We had better be going," Nell swiveled round to face the prince, "now, although I'm sure it was *lovely* to meet you, Prince – what was it again? - James, Hank and I must start making our way home."

James wrinkled his nose in annoyance as he replied, "Yes, *lovely* to meet you too, princess." Of course, neither of them was being entirely truthful, in fact, there was a hint of sarcasm in both of their voices. "Come on, Firestorm, we should get back to the castle," James snapped. As Princess Nell stomped towards the back of the clearing, the prince strode irately towards the front, assuming that Chuck the dragon was following him.

However, he turned around to find that his hunting pal was following the princess instead; apparently fascinated by her hair. A flash of irritation crossed James' eyes as he saw this. He called after the dragon, "Firestorm! Come *on!*" Chuck completely ignored his friend and carried on pottering after Nell and Hank. Feeling anger flare inside him, James stormed across the clearing and started furiously trying to shove the dragon in the opposite direction. "No, Firestorm, we're going *this* way!" he panted as he struggled to move Chuck. No matter how hard he tried, James could not move his dragon, who was now rooted to the spot and refusing to go one way or the other.

"It looks like your dragon wants to help us get home," winked Nell triumphantly.

"Not without me, he's not," huffed James. Nell and Hank looked at each other and rolled their eyes simultaneously. Hank squawked and sighed.

"I know right, Hank, *just great,*" Nell muttered sarcastically.

"I heard that!" protested Prince James resentfully. The four of them slowly started to trudge into the undergrowth toward the back of the clearing and Nell could already hear James moaning to Chuck about how unfair it was that he had to come along.

"It's going to be a long day," she muttered to herself, "a *very* long day."

5. Hunting

The sun had nearly reached its highest point in the sky over the impressive, emerald forest in which four unlikely companions were travelling. Nell, Hank, James and Chuck had made a reasonable amount of progress through the thick undergrowth of the woodland, having found a small dirt path to follow. However, as no one was entirely sure where they were going (though none would admit to it) and with the heat rising with the sun, the prince and princess were finding it difficult to get along.

"I can't believe you," snapped Nell, "You're *such* an ignoramus!" The princess stormed off ahead of the rest of the group to collect her thoughts and have some time to cool off. Hank chirped accusingly at Prince James and flew after Nell. The prince and Chuk fell in step a few paces behind. James felt frustrated that he didn't get the last word in the argument with the princess.

"Firestorm, why on Earth did you decide to follow this... this... GIRL? We could have been back at the castle eating breakfast and lunch by now." James moaned, turning to his dragon. As if on cue, James' stomach gurgled so loudly that it echoed around the trees. "See!" he protested, "I'm so hungry I could eat..." James thought for a moment, "I could eat a dragon!"

Chuck, who had been paying absolutely no attention to his whinging human until that point, stopped abruptly in his tracks and growled suspiciously at the prince. "Oh no, I wouldn't eat you, Firestorm!" James backtracked quickly, trying to placate the dragon, "It was just a slip of the tongue." Chuck snorted and a puff of smoke flew from his nostrils.
'I bet it was.' He thought sarcastically, not believing Prince James in the slightest. Slowly and apprehensively, Chuck

began to walk once again. James laughed at his friend and put an arm around the dragon's neck to reassure him. Chuck caved and nuzzled his human with a contented snort.

Meanwhile, just a few steps ahead, Princess Nell and Hank were deep in conversation. Hank was chirping incessantly in Nell's ear in worried and frantic tones. "Yes, I know," Nell replied quietly, "but how are we going to find a way out of here? We don't know where we are, how we got here or how to get back." The princess scuffed her feet hopelessly as she continued, "I feel like we're just walking around in circles in this forest!" Hank paused for a moment to consider all the facts. He chirped again, gesturing to James with his wing. *'Maybe, princess, we should ask the person who owns the kingdom!'* he thought grumpily, knowing that she had far too much pride to do such a thing.
"Oh, Hank, I know I should, but I just can't. I don't want his help and if we let him think we're lost then he will get all 'Prince Charming' on us again. I can't cope with that more than once in one day!" Nell sighed downtrodden. Both her and Hank agreed that they didn't want to witness the awfully awkward attempts of Prince James to be a hero again and so they carried on in a thoughtful silence. Nell, in a burst of frustration, muttered, "But what are we going to do? We *are* lost!"

At that moment, the prince and his dragon caught up with Nell and Hank on the path. Nell stopped talking immediately and started to blush, hoping that they hadn't heard her. James approached the princess, looking as though he wanted to say something. Nell thought he looked as though he needed the toilet and supressed the giggle which was rising in her throat. James coughed and finally began to speak, "Fleur... ah, that is, princess..."

Nell rolled her eyes, "What do *you* want?" James looked at the floor and twisted his feet in the dirt self-consciously, his golden hair falling over his eyes.

"I..." he started, brushing the rogue strands out of his face, "I feel that we, I mean, that I haven't made the best first impression. Perhaps we could start over?" James looked at her hopefully, his warm hazel eyes wide like a puppy as he waited for her reply.

Nell smirked as she answered, "If that's an apology then I'll think about accepting."

Without even thinking, a shocked James refused, "No, I'm not apologising! You're such a strong headed, annoying little..." James was interrupted by Chuck the dragon growling in annoyance at both of them for arguing again.

"Well fine," Nell huffed.

"Fine," James agreed.

"*Fine*," Nell finished, needing to have the last word.

Nell walked ahead, unimpressed, with Hank following her. James and Chuck returned to their original position a few steps behind the princess and they walked on in silence for a little while. Both the prince and princess were stewing on the conversation in their minds whilst they were walking. Neither one wanted to admit that they were in the wrong or that they were being childish and stubborn. All around them, the forest filled the silence with birds tweeting and singing glorious melodies, leaves rustling as the wind flowed through them like a river and water gushing over rocks and roots somewhere in the distance. James was the first to break through the forest's symphony by muttering to himself and Chuck. "I don't know who she thinks she is," he moaned as he ran his fingers through his tousled hair, "she's such a spoilt brat. She doesn't even *look* like a princess, I mean, look at her; she's a mess!"

"I can hear you know!" Nell shouted over her shoulder, frustrated. It was James' turn to blush now and his cheeks reddened as he realised he was not speaking as quietly as he thought. Nell continued to talk but to Hank who was hovering beside her as she walked, "He thinks he's so *charming*. He makes my blood boil!"

"You know, I can hear you too, princess," James called towards where she was walking. Nell rolled her eyes again (she thought this might become a recurring action).

"Do I look like I care, *Charming*?" she yelled, provoking a response.

"What did you call me?" James asked, his brow beginning to furrow.

"Charming," Nell replied sarcastically, trying to annoy the prince, "because you're just so *charming*." James was about to deliver a cutting comeback when he looked at Chuck. The dragon was eyeing him with a damning expression and James sighed.

"Okay, Firestorm, you win," he murmured reluctantly to his hunting pal.

Prince James started to jog to catch up to the princess. This time, he really intended to make amends, with a small prod from his dragon. He began quietly, so that she almost couldn't hear him, "Fleur, uh, princess."

"What is it now?" snapped Nell, still irritable from their previous conversation.

"Are you hungry? Because I'm starving and I'm sure your little bird friend could do with an energy boost," James asked, trying his best to sound cheery despite his mood. Chuck the dragon growled appreciatively at the mention of food and Hank joined in, chirping excitedly. Soon, all three pairs of eyes were on the princess, awaiting her answer.

Nell stopped walking and thought for a moment, her face deep in concentration. She sighed reluctantly before agreeing, "Alright, yes, I'm hungry. But where exactly can we find food in this forest? It's not just going to fall out of the sky!" At this, James perked up as he knew he could provide a solution.

"That's where Firestorm and I come in. We're..."

"Chuck," Nell interrupted, "his name is Chuck; stop being pretentious."

James carried on, irritated but ignoring the princess' interjection, "Firestorm and I are very good at hunting."

"Oh?" Nell asked, surprised.

"Yes, actually, we were mid-hunt when I came in to, er, rescue you," James paused for a moment then hastily carried on before the princess could comment, "so stay right here and we'll be back with food very shortly."

With that, James skilfully swung his leg over Chuck's back and the dragon began to take off. As they lifted above the trees, James called down to Nell and Hank, "I hope you like wild boar!" before swooping off into another part of the forest too quickly for Nell to follow. Princess Nell looked around her, found an upturned stump of an old tree and sat down to wait. She rested her chin on her hands, exhaustion starting to set in. Her eyes began to droop and her shoulders started to sag as she drifted off to somewhere into the corners of her consciousness.

*

As the princess opened her eyes, bright lights dazzled her from all around. She squinted and reached her hand to her brow to shade her face. The lights began to fade and she found herself back at home in the castle gardens. A wave of relief rushed over her; she was back at home and everything was normal. The whole ordeal in the forest must have been a bad dream. In the background, she could hear her parents talking and laughing somewhere in the castle and the servants rushed around her tidying and sorting as if she wasn't there.

Nell decided to head indoors and made her way towards the castle doors. Before she could reach them, a figure blocked her path. As she looked closer, she realised it was her childhood friend, Christopher. He hadn't aged at all since she last saw him. At first, she was elated as she still missed him. Her mind was buzzing with questions she needed answers to. But as she looked closer, she noticed that his face was void of expression, his eyes were dark and he was murmuring some kind of chant in a language which she didn't understand. He started to walk closer to her.

Nell shifted backwards on her feet, transfixed by the boy she thought she knew. "Kiff?" she said hesitantly, "Kiff, you're scaring me." The princess continued to step backwards as Christopher advanced on her, chanting continuously. Nell became more and more panicked and stumbled to the floor when her bad ankle gave way beneath her. "Help!" she cried out, but the castle staff carried on with their jobs as though they couldn't hear her. It was like she had ceased to exist.

The closer her old best friend got to her, the louder his chanting grew. Nell's eyes started to well with tears as the panic rose to her throat and she could no longer speak. She watched helplessly as Christopher reached her and began to crouch beside her, still chanting loudly. The garden suddenly caught ablaze; green flames seemed to surround her. His eyes were swirling with darkness and she felt herself being pulled into them. She tried with all her might to back away but it was no use, the darkness was too strong and it started to overwhelm her...

*

The princess woke with a start as Prince James and Chuck the dragon landed back on the path with an almighty gust of wind. On Chuck's back was a large boar which they had killed whilst out hunting. James jumped down from his dragon and landed skilfully on the grassy floor. He hauled the boar from Chuck's back and, using a loop of rope, attached it to the branch of a tree. James looked over to Nell with a triumphant smile on his face, unaware that she was still shaken from her dream. "So, princess, what do you think?" he grinned. Nell looked at him, her eyes still wet from the tears she cried in her sleep. She looked over at the boar and wrinkled her nose.

"How are we supposed to eat *that*?" she replied, completely unimpressed. James' facial expression changed. His brows furrowed and his smile disappeared.

"You always find the negative in everything, don't you?" he argued.

"Sorry, I didn't mean to come across ungrateful. I just..." Nell trailed off, leaving her sentence unfinished as she didn't want to admit that she was shaken by her dream.

James responded, a little shocked, "*Sorry?* I never thought I'd hear that word leave your mouth!" he started to smile again, "Don't worry, Firestorm will..."

"His name is Chuck," interjected Nell.

James completely ignored her and carried on, "*Firestorm* will sort that boar out. Will you do the honours, friend?"

The dragon rolled his eyes and blew a ball of flame over the boar, charring its skin and cooking it through. Nell's eyes grew wide as she saw the spectacle but, as she noticed the prince looking over at her, she cast her eyes to the ground and pretended not to be interested. James sighed despairingly and started to carve the meat of the boar with his sword. He carved two slices which he handed to Nell to eat. He also carved three slices for himself and a slice for Hank. Chuck looked at James expectantly. "Go on then,

Firestorm," James laughed, "the rest is for you." With an excited grunt, Chuck the dragon devoured the rest of the boar in one large gulp.

The rest of the group ate in silence. Once they had finished, James stood up and looked over at the sky. The afternoon sun had gone past the centre of the sky and was now beginning its half-day long descent towards the horizon. "Come on," he announced, "we had better keep walking if we want to get home before nightfall." Nell, Hank and Chuck stretched their limbs and stood up with James, ready to go. They continued to follow the path they had been walking previously. Within a short while, Nell and Hank had pulled slightly ahead of the prince and his dragon once again and they continued quietly, now full and content.

6. Waterfalls

By mid-afternoon, the four unlikely companions had relaxed a little. Nell and Hank were weaving in and out of trees, chasing each other and giggling whilst Chuck and James were walking side by side watching them. Chuck the dragon longed to join in the princess and her pet's game but he knew that James would be unhappy if he did. He puffed a small plume of smoke from his nostrils in annoyance. "What's the matter, Firestorm?" asked James, "You don't want to join those two do you? They're being so childish."

Chuck was about to roar in protest when they stumbled into a stunning clearing in the trees. James gasped as he gazed around the area in wonder. How had he never spotted this place before? The edges of the clearing were filled with lush grass and beautiful flowers of every colour. In the centre, a crystal-clear spring glistened with two tall and graceful waterfalls gushing and tumbling into its depths from a great height. Around the spring sprouted ferns and tiger lilies, which provided a frame for this magnificent picture. The prince had come to a complete stop, taking in the beauty that surrounded him. "Wow," he whispered breathlessly.

At that moment, Nell came running into the clearing, looking behind her to see how close Hank was following behind. As she wasn't looking where she was going, she crashed into James and rolled head over heels onto the floor. "Ouch!" cried Nell in pain.
"What do you think you're doing?" James demanded, picking himself up from the grass, "You can't keep still for one minute, can you?" He folded his arms crossly over his chest.

"It's not like I did it intentionally, Charming! In fact, I'd say *you* were in my way," Nell responded, shooting him an appalled look. She peered over at her ankle, which until this point was recovering well, to see that it was swollen and red once again. She groaned in a mixture of pain and annoyance. James noticed that she was hurt and, feeling a little bad, offered the princess his hand to help her up. Nell looked at his hand, chose to ignore it and pushed herself up using a nearby rock to support her weight.

Retracting his hand, James muttered to himself, "She's *such* a child."

"I heard that," snapped Nell.

Ignoring their bickering, the two animals flew over to the water and began to drink. Chuck took huge gulps of water, whereas Hank took small sips with his beak. Hank kept his distance from the dragon as he still didn't trust the creature. Chuck neither noticed nor cared as he was just excited to be able to drink clean, fresh water. Nell and James were stood silently watching their animal friends. "Well, Charming, shall we go and get a drink too? Or are you going to continue standing there open-mouthed?" prodded the princess.

"Oh, right, yes," replied James, disgruntled. He moved quietly over to the nearest edge of the pool. Nell followed a few steps behind. She had an inquisitive look on her face whilst she tried to figure out why the prince seemed so familiar. There was something about him that she couldn't pinpoint that, even though she found him the most annoying being on the planet, warmed her to him. It was as though she'd known him in another life.

When the prince and princess reached the spring, they both knelt and cupped their hands to take a drink. Nell continued to look at James, watching how his sandy hair fell over his eyes as he leant towards the water.

"What are you doing?" asked James, amused that he'd caught her looking at him.

Nell felt a fierce blush rise to the surface of her cheeks and replied quietly, "Nothing. I was just thinking."

"Thinking about what?" James questioned.

"None of your business, Charming!" retorted Nell, quickly shutting down any further questions James might have. Hank flew over to the princess and started to cheap and squeak at her, forming sentences. It was James' turn to stare as Nell understood the whole symphony of noises and was even able to reply, "Yes, I think you're right Hank. I guess I *am* a little grubby." Hank continued to chirp. "Do you think? Here?" asked Nell. Hank replied with a further sentence of twittering and Nell nodded, "Alright then, I suppose we might not find another place like this." James was entranced by the conversation between the princess and her bird.

Suddenly, Nell turned around. "Right!" she started, "Go away you two!"

James looked puzzled, "What?"

"The water is fresh and I need to wash," answered Nell, "now go away." Chuck the dragon, who had also heard the conversation from across the spring, didn't need to be told twice. He immediately flapped his wings and took off into the skies, leaving the princess in peace. Nell turned her attention to James, "Ahem."

"Ah yes, right then, I'll be back later," James replied awkwardly. He turned on his heel and hurried out of the clearing to leave Nell alone by the pool. Hank had fluttered into the branches of a nearby tree to give his friend some privacy. Now alone, Nell threw off her dress and jumped into the spring. The water was cool and refreshing; it felt good to wash after the last night and day of wandering the forest. She had been covered in dirt and bits of tree more times than she cared to count. The princess splashed and swum around in the pool and started to undo her braids so that she could wash her long, tangled hair.

Meanwhile, James had found a large tree on the edge of the clearing. With nothing better to do, he decided to climb the enormous oak and set about scaling its branches. Once he reached the middle of the old tree, he settled on a sturdy branch and lent against the trunk. Quite by accident, he saw that from the branch he could see directly into the clearing below. Almost immediately, his eyes were drawn to the slight figure in the spring. Nell was facing away from him, humming the same song which he had heard in the forest that morning. Her flowing auburn hair draped in wet tendrils down her spine. The prince had never noticed how vibrant her hair looked, but then it had always been laced with mud.

From the skies above, Chuck the dragon noticed his friend, James, sat on the tree branch. He was tired of flying and thought it would be kind of him to keep his human company. He swooped down and gracefully landed on the branch next to the prince. James looked around to see his dragon sitting next to him and his eyes widened. "Firestorm, you can't sit on this, it won't hold your weight!" he exclaimed in hushed tones so that the princess wouldn't hear him. Chuck was about to snort in protest when they both heard a huge crack coming from the base of the branch. Without a second warning, the branch began to plummet taking the dragon and prince down with it. Chuck opened his wings, allowing him to glide to land on the edge of the clearing. But James had no such luxury. He landed with a large splash in the middle of the spring.

Nell heard the splash and looked over her shoulder. Seeing James, soaking wet, in the middle of the pool, she screamed. The princess lunged for the bank, keeping herself submerged in the water. "Hank!" she yelled and the hawk soared down to her with her dress. Nell's cheeks flushed a deep red with anger and embarrassment as she grabbed her dress and ran behind a nearby willow tree. Chuck, who was sat on the grass at the edge of the clearing, covered his eyes with his ears. James didn't know where to look so he put his hands over his face. "What are you doing in here?" shouted Nell.

"I... um..." stuttered James, "I'm sorry, princess. I was climbing a tree, looking for fruit, when I misplaced my foot and the branch snapped." Chuck gratefully noticed that James had not mentioned his part in the accident and lifted one ear to see if it was now safe to look. As he realised Nell was now back in her dress and standing in front of the willow tree, Chuck snorted in relief. James heard this and uncovered his own eyes. The prince looked anywhere and everywhere but at Princess Nell as he climbed out of the spring and ran, dripping, out of the clearing.

"You know, Hank, I'm sure there aren't any fruit trees in this clearing," Nell muttered, suspiciously. '*How charming*,' she thought to herself.

7. The Search

Back in the kingdom of Sundragon, chaos and panic had taken hold. The princess had been gone for the night and almost an entire day since the dragon had flown away with her. The king and queen had sent out multiple search parties with no luck thus far and were waiting for any news of their precious daughter. In the great hall, King Robert and Queen Lydia stood together, holding hands. They pressed their foreheads to each other's, both hoping for a miracle. The arched door creaked open slowly and both monarchs looked up sharply. A knight entered the room. "Well?" asked King Robert, the strain and anxiety of the situation apparent in his voice. The knight shook his head solemnly.

"Nothing yet, your highness," he replied. Queen Lydia buried her head in her husband's shoulder, stifling a sob.

"Then get back to it, man!" the king ordered, "And don't stop until you find her!"

"Yes, your highness, of course," the knight agreed and bowed his head as he left the couple alone in the grand dining hall. He went back to join the hundreds of soldiers and civilians out searching the kingdom for the missing princess.

Queen Lydia lifted her head from her husband's shoulder and delicately wiped a tear from her cheek. "Oh Robert," she sighed, "she will come home, won't she?" The queen looked Robert in the eyes, her own glistening with tears. He met her gaze warmly and tried to reassure his wife in such a difficult time.

"Of course, Lydia, she will be home soon enough," he soothed.

"But Robert, this will be her second night out there alone. She's a princess, she's not used to the forests. What if..."

The king interrupted, "Now Lydia, we can't think like that. Nell will be okay; she has to be." They returned to their position; holding hands and resting their foreheads against one another's waiting for news of their daughter as the sun started to fall below the horizon.

8. Secrets

Somewhere deep in the forest under the sapphire blue night sky, the four travellers had found a spot to rest for the night. They had come across the cave as the sun was setting and Chuck had searched the whole thing first to be sure it was safe. The small cave was scattered with plants baring luminescent flower buds, bathing the area in a rosy glow. James had built a little campfire in the centre of the shelter for warmth and they had settled down to sleep. Hank was perched on a jutting rock at the edge of the cave. James lay on a pile of leaves on the cave floor with his cape for a blanket and resting his head on Chuck's tail. Chuck curled around James to keep his friend warm and closed his eyes.

Whilst the others slept, Nell sat with her back against a rock, watching the prince and his dragon. Her mind was filled with the events of the day and she thought of her parents back at home. Her heart ached for them and she longed to tell them that she was okay. Suddenly, she had an idea. "Chuck," she whispered to the dragon. When she got no reply, she nudged his shoulder and whispered again, slightly louder, "Chuck!" The dragon opened one eye sleepily and saw Nell waiting for him to wake up. He lifted his head from the floor and tilted it to one side to show her he was listening. "I have a favour to ask of you, do you think you could help me?" she asked. Chuck snorted quietly in agreement, so the princess continued with a sigh, "I'm lost, Chuck. I woke up in the forest this morning and I don't remember how I got there. I don't even know what happened yesterday. I have no idea which direction we should be travelling in and I haven't got a clue where I am. I can't tell James because I don't want his help; I don't want him to feel sorry for me," Nell pauses to swallow a sob, "do you think you could fly me above the trees so I know how to get home?"

Chuck slowly and carefully moved his tail from under James' head and padded over to Nell. He nuzzled her face and lowered himself to the floor so that she could climb on. The princess gingerly clambered onto his back and wrapped her arms tightly around his neck. When the dragon thought that Nell was ready, he gave a great flap of his wings and took off into the skies, soaring above the clouds. Nell had never experienced anything like this before. She was elated and overwhelmed by the beauty of the view all around her. They were surrounded by a sea of shining stars glittering in the night sky. The tops of the trees swayed gently in the calm breeze and the moon shone brightly in the centre of the sky. Nell felt so close she might be able to touch it if she reached out her hand. Then she saw it, her castle. The silhouette of the great building hung in the horizon not far from the direction in which they had been travelling. Relief rushed over her.

*

Back on the ground, James sat up and gazed towards the sky. The movement of air created by Chuck's wings had woken him up and he saw his dragon and the princess fly up into the sky. James began to wonder where the princess had come from; he had never heard of a Princess Fleur before but she seemed familiar. He recognised her smile from somewhere, but he didn't know why. Her laugh sounded like something from a dream when he heard her playing with Hank earlier in the day. The prince lay back down and waited for them to return to the ground.

*

As she began to feel a little braver in the sky, Nell sat up on Chuck's back and took in the sensations of flying. She reached to stroke Chuck's forehead and, as she did, something unusual happened. Her eyes went blurry and she could see circles and bright lights in the centre of her vision. The princess blinked in surprise and when she opened her eyes again, the world looked different. She was able to zoom in on the smallest creature on the forest floor and could see clearly even though it was the middle of the night and they were surrounded by darkness. Without explanation, she heard a voice in her head. *'Now you can see what I see.'*

"What?" Nell asked, shocked.

The voice spoke again, *'We have formed a bond. Now when you ride me, you can see through the eyes of a dragon.'*

"Chuck? Is that you? I mean, I can understand you when you speak but, how are you in my head?" she continued, perplexed.

'The bond between a Sundragon and your family is unbreakable. We have always existed together. Now you have flown on my back, we can communicate this way.'

"My family?" questioned Nell, "But, we've never had dragons in the kingdom..."

A fierce gust of wind blew over them. Nell shivered. Chuck started to descend back to the cave, through the treetops. *'You're tired,'* he soothed, *'we should return to the cave to rest.'* With that, the dragon landed on the soft, grassy, forest floor and tipped Nell off his back. He then nudged her with his head towards the cave.

Whilst they were settling back down, Nell turned to Chuck and started to talk, not realising that Prince James was awake and could hear every word. "Chuck, can I tell you something?" Nell murmured. Chuck nodded in agreement and rested his head on her lap encouragingly. "Well, I haven't been entirely honest with Prince Charming over there. I haven't told him where I'm from or even my real name. You see, I didn't know if I could trust him. You already know that I am the princess of Sundragon, well, my name is Princess Elenore – Nell for short." James' eyes widened as he heard Nell's name for the first time, but he remained completely still. She continued, "I think I've realised that the reason I can't warm to James is because he reminds me of someone I once knew back at my home. He was called Christopher, but I called him Kiff. He was my best friend, Chuck. We spent every day together until I was seven and he had to go away. We wrote to each other for three and a half years then, one day, his letters just stopped. I don't know why he stopped writing and, to this day, it breaks my heart every time I think of it. He was the only friend I ever had, except Hank of course, and he was gone with no explanation. I've never quite managed to get past it." Nell looked at Chuck, tears threatening to spill over her eyelids.

Unknown to Nell, James had heard every single word. They had pierced his heart. His face was scrunched tight like a piece of paper and it took every ounce of his strength not to allow the tears to fall himself. He could never tell her, no matter how much he wanted to. It would always be his secret.

Nell swallowed hard before speaking again, "Thank you for letting me talk to you, Chuck. I've never spoken to anyone about it before. When it happened, everyone just pretended like everything was normal apart from me and I could never talk to anyone about it. I feel a bit better now. Goodnight, Chuck." Chuck snorted and lifted his head. He padded round the cave and James quickly relaxed his face so the dragon wouldn't notice he was awake. He curled up around James as before but left his tail next to the princess so she could use it as a pillow. Nell leant on it and quickly fell asleep.

Once Chuck's breathing had settled indicating he had also drifted off, James sat up once again. His mind raced with the secret he had just overheard. She had lied about who she was. She was from *Sundragon*, the sworn enemy of his family's kingdom. And yet, for reasons he could never tell, hearing the secret had left him feeling almost as heartbroken as the princess herself. For the rest of the night, James tossed and turned, unable to sleep well. He awoke many times before the morning and was the victim of more than one bad dream.

9. Near Miss

As the sun was still rising, Princess Nell was woken by an almighty crash at the back of the cave. She sat upright, startled by the noise, and looked around to see where it had come from. All of a sudden, Hank collided with her chest, looking dazed. Nell followed his line of travel to see Chuck the dragon snorting triumphantly and Prince James running up behind him breathlessly. "Firestorm, that's *not* how you play tig! You can't just throw the baby bird across the cave!" James shouted. Chuck roared unhappily but settled down quickly as, in reality, he knew he was in the wrong.

Nell smiled at the little argument that had unfolded in front of her and then she realised she had her baby hawk still bundled on her chest. Her eyes softened as she looked down at him and cooed, "Oh Hank, you are silly. That didn't end so well, did it?" she laughed and continued, "That'll teach you for playing tig with a dragon!" Nell stroked Hank's head as he chirped quietly and she nuzzled him close to her. Feeling a little better, Hank hopped onto his human's shoulder. The princess ran her hands through her clean, glossy, auburn hair and re-braided it skilfully as Prince James approached.

James started to speak as he got closer, "We should get going now if you want to get home today, Princess Fleur." James remembered Nell's conversation with his dragon last night. He must still call her by the name she gave him, or she'd know he had heard everything. When he reached the princess, he offered her his hand to help her up and, just like the day before, she ignored his hand and got up by herself. James' face flushed pink with annoyance and he continued talking, "So, which direction are we taking today, *princess?*" Nell took a breath to answer, but James cut her off, "Actually, I've been thinking."

"That's dangerous," mused Nell with a smirk lingering at the corners of her mouth.

James ignored her and carried on, "I don't know why I didn't think of it before, really. We have a dragon."

"Your point is?" queried Nell.

James replied, getting more irritated with each interruption, "So why don't we just fly you home? It would be much quicker and then we can all get on with our own separate lives."

The princess looked James in the eyes, feeling stung. She tried not to give her emotions away and quickly masked her face with a frown. She had started to become a little fonder of Prince James and had thought that he might have felt the same. Nell scolded herself for being so foolish and the emotional barriers which she had started to drop were built back up immediately. "The sooner the better," she muttered sharply, still reprimanding herself for allowing her emotions to play a part. As Chuck began to kneel down to allow James and Nell to climb on his back, Princess Nell was struck by a thought. "This is not a good idea. It won't work," she said.

James looked at her, puzzled, "And why won't it?"

Nell thought how best to word her answer, "My parents have an aversion to dragons – I don't know why. If we flew in on a dragon they would have a heart attack and they'd probably send the entire army after us. I couldn't bare it if Chuck got hurt."

"Ah, I see. No, I would prefer it if *Firestorm* was not attacked by an army," James snapped, "walking it is then. We'd better get moving as I'm guessing we've a long way to go."

"You guessed right," replied Nell.

"How *did* you get out here anyway?" asked James.

"It might sound weird," Nell mumbled, "but I don't actually remember." Before the prince had a chance to respond or ask any more questions, Nell had walked ahead with Hank like the day before.

James sighed and said to his dragon, "I don't understand that girl. How can you not know how you got somewhere?" Chuck snorted as though he couldn't care less and the two carried on in a comfortable silence for a while.

Meanwhile, at the front of the party, Nell was telling Hank about what she had seen the previous night. "I saw our castle, Hank," she whispered, "last night." Hank squeaked excitedly, asking for more detail. "Really, I did! Chuck took me up above the trees so I could see where we needed to go. We're not lost anymore, Hank, we're going in the right direction." Hank chirped happily and perched on the princess' shoulder. Nell thought about what had happened between her and the dragon that evening, the bond they had formed and how she could see through his eyes. "Oh and..." she started. Hank looked at her, waiting for her to carry on. At the last moment, Nell thought it better not to tell Hank about her experience, "never mind, it's not important. What's important is that we're going home!" Hank squeaked in agreement and they continued travelling in a happy and peaceful state.

A few steps behind Nell and Hank, James was moaning once again about the princess. Chuck, who was fed up with hearing what sounded like a broken record, was ignoring his human completely and not even pretending to be interested. Still, this didn't stop the prince, "I mean, why does she have to be so ignorant? Did you see what she did earlier, Firestorm?" Chuck rolled his eyes and continued to ignore his friend. James carried on, "I offered her my hand, *again,* and she just ignored it like it wasn't even there. Then she looked at me like I was the one being rude!" he got a little more wound up and raised his voice, "And then there's the fact that she keeps calling you *Chuck,* I mean, what a stupid name!" Chuck stopped abruptly and roared at James, offended. "Oh, don't tell me you like it, Firestorm. This is ridiculous."

"Don't insult his name," called Nell from just ahead of them, "it's not Chuck's fault you have no taste; Firestorm indeed!" James looked over both offended at the princess' comment and a little sheepishly as he didn't realise that he was talking that loudly. He only hoped that she hadn't heard him moaning about her as well.

The Princess stopped in her tracks. She looked at Hank and then turned around to James and his dragon. "Did any of you hear that?" she asked, tentatively.

"Hear what, princess?" asked James. Nell pointed towards the trees up ahead.

"There was a rustling and crunching noise coming from those trees just now," Nell explained. Hank squeaked anxiously whilst James looked at the trees thoughtfully.

With one eyebrow raised, he replied arrogantly, "I'm sure it's nothing. No one would want to follow us here in *my* forest." Chuck grunted in agreement with his friend as he didn't know why anyone would try to follow a *dragon* if they wanted to live.

"Are you sure, Charming?" Nell replied with a sly grin, "If you're this pretentious with everyone you meet I think a fair few might do so." James tutted but did not react to the princess' jibe. "Oh fine, we'll keep going," sighed Nell, "you're no fun."

The group carried on walking though Nell and Hank were very much on edge. They continuously scoured the trees and undergrowth around the path for signs of movement. Suddenly, from the branches above the travellers, a deafening crack filled the forest. Nell jumped, frightened and yelled, "What was *that*?" Hank flew under Nell's hair and hid next to her braid. Prince James laughed conceitedly.

"Really, princess, I don't know why you're so worried. It was obviously just a bird in the trees above us. The people of my kingdom love me; no one will harm us," he said, brushing off Nell's panic.

"If you don't drop the arrogant idiot act, I might harm you in a minute," she muttered to herself. Then, to James, she said reluctantly, "Fine, if you're so confident then you and your dragon can walk ahead. Hank and I will drop back. We just need to keep walking straight, *if* you can manage that."

"Sure," James replied, "if it helps you realise that there's absolutely nothing to worry about."

The prince and Chuck headed in front and Nell fell behind them with Hank still on her shoulder, hiding in her hair. "Well isn't he full of himself!" the princess whispered to Hank, who chirped in her ear in agreement. They all continued on towards Nell's castle, exhausted from travel and a terrible night's sleep. As they progressed further, the trees became more and more spaced out as though the forest was thinning. Nell was still checking the undergrowth for any signs of danger and didn't notice that James and Chuck had come to a stop ahead of her. she walked straight into the back of the prince, sending both of them flying to the mossy floor. They lay sprawled on the floor, groaning for a few moments before trying to sit up. The groans got louder from James as he found his feet and he opened his mouth to start an argument.

Before he could say a word, Chuck the dragon let out a loud, short roar and interrupted. Their gaze was drawn forwards towards him and they gasped in wonder as they saw what lay beyond him. A gigantic, blood orange canyon of deadly drops, incredible peaks and rock formations panned out in front of them. It stretched as far as the horizon; they couldn't see the other side. "Woah," Nell uttered under her breath.

"Yeah, woah," James agreed, astounded. The four adventurers simply stood there motionless for a few moments, taking in the view.

Unexpectedly, a concerned Hank fluttered in front of Nell's face and started squeaking incessantly. "Hang on a minute, Hank," Nell said, "you know I can't understand you when you speak that quickly!" Hank paused for a minute before squeaking in the same tones again, only a little slower this time. "Oh, I see. Yes, you do have a point," replied Nell. James looked at the princess and the hawk in confusion. "What's he saying?" he asked. Nell ignored James, much to his annoyance, and continued to converse with Hank.

"Right, Hank, but that could take a very long time. And how do we know that there even *is* a way around it?" she queried. James became impatient and shouted loudly, "Princess! What is he saying?" Princess Nell turned to James and gave him a withering look.

"If you had let me finish my conversation with Hank," she said, "I would have told you anyway. Hank thinks we should walk around the canyon." James looked at Nell as if she had lost her mind.

"Why walk when you can fly?" he grinned. Chuck snorted in approval, eager to stretch his wings after all the walking.

Nell looked at Hank, who was fluttering around anxiously, then at Chuck and James. She considered all the options; how long it might take to walk around the ravine, if they *could* get around it, how much quicker it would be to fly, the risks of flying. In the end, she thought the benefits outweighed the risks. "Okay, I hate to say this but I agree with Charming on this one. We'll have to stay low but, Hank, who knows if we could even walk around this thing. It's huge!" she announced.

James said triumphantly, "I knew you'd see sense eventually and realise that..."

"Don't get carried away, Charming," Nell cut in, "you're only right this once. I still don't like you." The princess turned her back on James to calm Hank as he was still panicking about the flight. James sighed at her stubbornness and looked at Chuck, who was already kneeling down and waiting for the humans to get on so he could fly. "Alright, buddy, let's get going," James laughed, climbing onto the dragons back. "*Princess*," he continued, "are you coming or what?" Nell huffed and climbed on behind the prince.

"Now this is just so I don't fall off," she warned whilst wrapping her hands around James' waist, "so don't get any ideas!" James feigned offence in his expression as he looked at her but there was a clear smile twitching at the corners of his mouth. He turned back around away from Nell before she could see his smile starting to spread.

There was a sudden jolt as Chuck started to take off, flapping his powerful, golden wings and lifting off the ground. Nell, thinking that James was asleep during her flight with Chuck last night, feigned surprise at the feeling of flying. "Wow! This is... this is magical!" she exclaimed. Chuck roared happily at the feeling of being back in the sky and James couldn't help but laugh.

"Now *this* is the way to travel!" he shouted over the noise of the wind which had picked up as they had begun crossing the canyon. Chuck glided effortlessly through the wind and further over the ravine with the two humans on his back. Hank was struggling to keep up, flapping alongside the dragon. Nell noticed this and cupped him in her hands so that he could sit on her shoulder instead. Hank chirped gratefully as he tried to get his breath back. As they continued to fly, the princess gazed around her, taking in the incredible scenery. She couldn't believe the stark contrast of the lush, emerald green forests they had emerged from and the deep, dry, orange canyon beneath them. The morning sun sat warmly in a clear blue sky and bounced of the sheer cliff edges below, creating pools of light in the crevices. It was terrifyingly beautiful.

As they reached around half-way across the canyon, Nell noticed what looked like a large bird coming towards them. "Charming," she started, "what's that?"

"What's what?" asked James, turning to look where she was pointing. The object was getting closer by the second, hurtling at horrifying speed.

"That!" cried the princess.

"Firestorm! DRAGON!" yelled James. Chuck looked to his left and saw the dragon pelting towards them. He quickly dove down to alter his flight path and avoid the creature, taking everyone by surprise and knocking them off balance. Luckily, the blood red dragon sped past just above their heads. Nell followed it as it flew away. It didn't turn around. Relieved, Nell pushed herself up from where she had fallen on Chuck's back. Something was missing.

"Chuck, have you seen Charming?" she asked, hesitantly, almost expecting him to jump from behind her and scare her. When he did no such thing, she began to call out for him, "Charming? Charming! Chuck, I don't see him anywhere! We haven't lost him, have we? Hank, can you see him?" The baby hawk flew around the dragon, trying to find the missing prince. He started tweeting loudly to the right side of Chuck, just underneath his stomach. Nell peered over the edge of the dragon to see James gripping tightly onto Chuck's foot with both hands. Beneath him was at least a hundred-foot drop. James' dagger slipped out of his pocket and plummeted towards the canyon floor. After what seemed like forever, he heard the sharp clang of metal as it splintered, hitting the jagged rocks below. The prince gulped. "Charming!" Nell called, secretly thankful that he was still alive. She leant towards him and stretched her arm as far as it would reach. "Grab onto my hand!" she shouted as James dangled perilously, his grip getting weaker.

James let go of the foot with one hand and swung his arm up towards Nell. His hand reached for hers but only brushed her fingertips. Off balance, James winced with the effort. He could feel the hold of his other hand loosening. "I can't keep holding on!" he called. Suddenly, Nell's mind took her back to the day at the treehouse, when she was the one who couldn't hold on and Christopher couldn't save her. She shook her head, that wasn't how this was going to go.

"Try again, once more, Charming!" shouted Nell, stretching even further down the side of the dragon. With his last remaining ounce of strength, James used all his weight to swing his hand up once again and grabbed the first thing it encountered. Thankfully, that object was the princess' outstretched arm and she wrapped her fingers around his wrist. Using both hands, Nell hauled with all her might and managed to get James up onto Chuck's back. The prince threw his leg over and, with Nell's help, managed to return to a secure sitting position astride the dragon.

Without thinking, Nell wrapped her arms tightly around James' waist to keep him steady. James gasped with surprise. "Have I hurt you?" Nell asked, worried.

"No, not at all," James replied, a grin starting to emerge, "I just wasn't expecting you to do that."

"Just in case you decide to fall off again," joked Nell.

"Sorry princess, you can't get rid of me that easily!" laughed James, feeling light-headed now that his body was filled with excess adrenaline.

Extremely quietly, in almost a whisper, Nell said, "I'm really glad you're alright." James didn't respond to this as he wasn't sure it was meant for his ears.

The travellers spent the rest of the flight in silence aside from the sound of their heavy breathing. When they finally landed on the other side of the ravine, Nell and James rolled off

Chuck's back and collapsed in a heap on the floor. "Boy does it feel good to be back on solid ground," said James.

Whilst she lay on her back, staring at the sky and gathering her thoughts, Nell wondered aloud, "Where do you think that dragon came from?" James was as puzzled about the incident as she was.

"I... really don't know," he admitted.

"Charming, are there often dragons flying around your kingdom? We don't see any in mine," Nell asked.

"Well," James said, thinking as he spoke, "there are lots of dragons but they usually stay in the mountains. I've never seen one this far out before – apart from Firestorm of course. And I've never seen them that aggressive."

"That's weird..." the princess paused for a moment, "well, we'd better get going again! I must be getting close to home by now!"

The pair stood up, not realising how close they were, and ended up inches away from each other with their noses almost touching. Nell gasped as she noticed the proximity of the prince. Gently, he brushed the hair out of her face and looked searchingly into her ice blue eyes as if he needed to ask her something. "James..." Nell started as their faces inched towards each other. His hand cupped her chin and his warm hazel eyes felt like they were looking straight through her exterior to find the answers he sought. They felt so familiar. Hank covered his face with his wing, blushing at the sight of them so close (if birds can blush). Just as Nell closed her eyes, Chuck snorted loudly and disapprovingly. Hearing the sudden noise broke the spell and both James and Nell jumped backwards, landing back in reality. Nell's cheeks flushed red and the prince looked awkwardly at the floor, not wanting to meet her eyes. "We should get going," muttered the princess, feeling embarrassed.

"Yes, let's go," said James hurriedly, still staring at the floor.

Chuck rolled his eyes as the group started walking once again, getting ever closer to Ned's castle. In fact, it now loomed as an ever-present shadow on the horizon, beyond the forest and much closer than before. She was nearly home.

*

Deep in a neighbouring forest, atop a towering mountain range, a wide plateau was bathed in the midday sun. To the left of the plateau was a deep red, canvas tent and a bonfire from which an unnatural smoke was billowing. The smoke was a deep grey with green flashes of light popping and crackling around it. Beside the fire stood a tall, dark haired man, gazing into the flames. His eyes sparkled, reflecting the green sparks and he had a menacing grin on his face.

To the left of the fire, the blood red dragon which attacked the travellers landed noiselessly. It lay down, cowering in fear. "Well?" the man demanded, "Where are they?" The dragon whimpered and grunted a few times. "What do you mean *they got away?*" he replied, in low, terrifying tones. His posture began to change. The man's shoulders broadened and he stood over the dragon intimidatingly. The dragon bowed its head, scared. "I give you one task on your own and you disappoint me like this!" bellowed the man, "Get out of my sight!" He started to hurl green bolts of lightning at the dragon and, though the creature dodged the electricity, it did not leave. Instead it roared louder. "What?" the man paused, "what do you mean a *sun* dragon? I haven't seen one of those since... wait, it *must* be." The petrifying figure thought for a moment, forming a plan in his mind. "YOU!" he yelled, pointing at the poor dragon on the floor, "Show me where you saw them. I will have the girl *and* the sun dragon, no matter what I have to destroy to get them." The man jumped onto the whimpering dragon's back and kicked it in the sides. As they took off, his chilling laugh could be heard echoing across the mountains.

10. Skyrain

In another castle, not far from the forest in which James and Nell were travelling, King Alfred and Queen Minerva were having afternoon tea. They were sat at a delicately decorated metal table in the shade of the impressive building. The castle was made of dark blue stones which made it look like the night sky. Large blue flags billowed above the turrets, swirling like shooting stars. The king and queen were discussing the fact that their son had not returned from his hunt the previous day. "I don't know, Alfred," Queen Minerva fretted, "James never usually stays out on a hunt unless he's told us first."

"I'm sure he's just lost track of time, Minerva," comforted the king.

"But he's never gone this long. What if he's in trouble? What if he's hurt?" she worried, her voice rising in panic as she considered the worst.

"Minerva, calm yourself!" King Alfred exclaimed, "You know James; he's probably found a whole herd of wild boar and will arrive home tomorrow with Firestorm triumphant as ever." King Alfred placed a tender arm around the queen's shoulders. Queen Minerva sighed.

"Oh, you're probably right my darling," she admitted, somewhat defeated.

The king smiled victoriously whilst giving his wife a gentle squeeze to reassure her. The slight crease of a frown still lingered on Queen Minerva's brow. "Though," she started, "it wouldn't hurt to send a few soldiers just to check on him; to make sure he's alright."

"Minerva," the king warned.

"Now, my love, don't you think it would be sensible especially with the recent sightings of *dragons* in the forest," she continued, ignoring the king's interjection. King Alfred's eyes widened at the mention of dragons and he hurriedly returned to his seat at the small, intricate table.

"I suppose you're right," he sighed, resigning himself to defeat once again. "we really should check that he's alright now that the dragons are away from the mountains. I shall send a group of guards to report on his wellbeing at once." Minerva smiled knowingly. She always knew how to win a debate with her husband but this was one she felt very strongly about. She knew her own son. Her son *always* told her if he would be away for any length of time. "Thank you, Alfred. I will feel much better knowing he's safe," she gushed gratefully to the king. She finished the last bite of the expertly crafted cake in her hand and dabbed her mouth politely with an embellished napkin.

King Alfred, somewhat reluctantly, called to a nearby attendant. He asked the servant to send for his captain of the guard and a few others. The man ran away hastily and shortly returned with five men behind him, dressed in grey and blue armour with shooting stars engraved in their chest plates. One man, who had mouse-brown hair and a shock of gold in his irises, also wore a royal blue cape with a silver clasp. The gentleman stepped forward and greeted the king, "Your highness." He bowed slightly and gave a graceful nod to the queen.

"Ah, Benedict, it's good to see you," the king smiled. He stood up and embraced his captain of the guard. Benedict returned the embrace before turning his attention to the matter at hand.

"You called me here about the prince, your highness?" he asked.

"Yes, my friend. The Queen is worried about her son as he has been away for longer than expected. He's probably fine, but with the sightings of dragons out of the mountains, she would like to confirm his safety," the king replied.

"Of course, your highness, I understand. We will locate the prince and return to confirm his wellbeing," Benedict nodded and turned on his heel to return to the other guards.

"Oh, and Benedict?" the king interrupted. The captain of the guard paused and looked over his shoulder.

"Sir?"

"You and your team should remain extra alert too. The dragons are unpredictable at the best of times and now they are in our territory. Who knows what they could do? Be careful, my friend."

"Of course, we will be vigilant. Thank you, your highness." With that, Benedict and his team walked quickly out of the castle and into the castle courtyard. They mounted their horses and rode through the kingdom, out into the forest beyond.

Still in the castle at their table, the king and queen resumed their afternoon tea. "I do hope they find him, Alfred," Queen Minerva quivered.

"Don't worry, my love, I'm sure he's perfectly safe," the king reassured. Little did they know that Prince James had found much more than a herd of boar in the forest this time.

11. Kidnapped

Somewhere within the same forest that the guards of both kingdoms were currently searching, Nell and James were still walking. They were edging ever closer to Nell's kingdom but were still unable to agree on anything. They had recently reached a fork in the path and were arguing relentlessly about which route to take. The dragon and hawk did not want to get involved and so hovered a short distance away, avoiding the confrontation. Hank was perched nervously on Chuck the dragon's head. Neither of them dared go any closer whilst their humans were shouting at each other. Nell was trying to make James understand that her route was preferable by shouting, "This way looks easier! It's much lighter and the path is much straighter. You're just trying to get us all lost!" She looked at the two paths. The one she had chosen, where the light was glittering through the gaps in the trees, bathing the grass in a dappled sunbeam, was relatively straight and looked like a smooth journey.

"Why are you so stubborn?" James yelled angrily, "I know *my* kingdom and I know my way out of it! Your way will take us in a circle. *My way* will get us out of here!"

Nell looked down the path along which James was pointing. It was dark with no light filtering through the thick canopy of leaves overhead. There were branches hanging low from the towering trees and the path was winding and uneven, with tree roots protruding from the ground. "You know what, go ahead!" she shouted, "You go that way if you want but I'm not coming with you. I'm not going *anywhere* until you stop being a bonehead!"

"Fine!" spat James.

"Fine!" Nell sat on the forest floor in a huff and crossed her arms. Prince James stormed down the path he had chosen without another word to the princess and with not so much as a look back to see if anyone else was following him.

Once James was out of sight, Chuck the dragon and Hank shuffled forwards towards the princess. They looked at Nell, at the path down which James had walked and then at each other, bemused. They didn't know what to do. Hank fluttered over to the princes and sat on her lap. He chirped, unsure, and tilted his head as if asking what they should do. "Don't worry about me Hank. Just give me a minute to cool off and I'll catch you up," Nell urged, stroking Hanks feathers. He looked at her quizzically. "Go!" she repeated. With one last look, Nell's pet hawk flapped away, following the root which Prince James had taken. Chuck the dragon plodded over to Nell, placed his head on her lap and snorted stubbornly as if to say, 'I'm not going anywhere.' "You too, Chuck." She insisted. Chuck snorted and refused to move. "Oh, well okay then. Thanks, Chuck. We'll catch them up in a minute. Let's just sit here for a little longer and give *Charming* the chance to calm down."

A little further up the darkened path, James was slowly trudging along. Hank was hovering at his shoulder. James sighed, "I don't know, Hank. I shouldn't have shouted at her like that. She's just *so* stubborn and she knows exactly which buttons to push to wind me up." Hank chirped, acknowledging the princess' stubbornness and perched on James' shoulder. James' eyes widened, momentarily surprised, as he realised that Hank was finally accepting him as a trustworthy human. "I mean," he continued, "I was right. This *is* a better way to go but maybe I should have..." Suddenly, without warning, a thunderous CRACK came from the leafy canopy above. Both James and Hank jumped from the noise. They started peering into the trees above them, trying to figure out where the noise had come from.

By the fork in the path, Chuck the dragon's ears pricked up, alert. He took the corner of Nell's dress in his mouth and began to tug at it urgently. "What is it, Chuck?" Nell asked, puzzled by his sudden change in behaviour.

Chuck roared deafeningly in a panic, yelling, *'We have to move, princess. Something's coming and it isn't anything good!'*

"Right now?" murmured the princess, still a little confused, "well okay then."

As Nell stood up to move along the path down which Prince James had stormed off, a dark blur of a shadow buzzed past her. Before she knew what was happening, the princess was knocked off her feet by the same fierce beast that had barrelled into the party mid-flight over the ravine. "Chuck!" she yelped, as the intimidating dragon towered over her where she fell, teeth bared and ready for another attack. Chuck heard Nell's cry for help and launched himself at the blood dragon, sending them both tumbling across the forest. The ruby red dragon winced as it was thrown up against an ancient oak tree but soon recovered and ran towards the princess once more. *'Hide, princess!'* roared Chuck as he threw himself in front of her once again to fend off the aggressor. Nell stumbled to the large log on which she had originally been sat and tucked herself behind it, making herself as small as she physically could. She couldn't see what was happening from behind the log so, instead, she squeezed her eyes closed and hoped for the best.

The two dragons fought for a long while, destroying the forest around them as they went. Nothing was safe; trees snapped and fell; bushes were burnt as the dark dragon seared scorching hot flames towards Chuck and the forest floor was filled with smoke. The unknown dragon was becoming increasingly unsettled as the flames it was breathing towards Chuck seemed to be making no dent.

Chuck was able to withstand an incredibly high heat – though he was not entirely aware of his own strength yet. Whilst the dragon was distracted, Chuck launched his own blast of blistering blue flames towards it, engulfing it in a ball of fire. This attack forced the scarlet dragon back towards the fork in the path and, unbeknownst to Nell, closer to the log behind which she was hiding. With a swift swing of its tail, the challenger knocked the log easily to one side and Nell was thrown violently across the forest floor. Upon landing, she hit her head on a rock and was knocked unconscious. Chuck noticed her lying motionless on the floor and was momentarily distracted from the fight. The other dragon saw its chance and backed Chuck into a corner, wearing him down with blow after blow. Chuck could hold out no more, as he was only a young dragon, and collapsed on the floor exhausted.

At this moment, the large dragon roared loudly to the skies above, as if calling for someone. Chuck squinted through weak eyes to see four smaller dragons emerging from the surrounding trees. They each had a corner of a huge net held in their mouths. The commanding dragon – the one which had fought Chuck – glided over to Nell, picked her up in one of its talons and threw her down next to Chuck. She bounced against Chuck's leg and stirred from her unconsciousness as the other dragons pulled up the corners of the net and began to flap their wings. The lead dragon flew ahead to scout for potential threats. As the dragons took off, carrying Nell and Chuck in their net, Nell turned to Chuck and mumbled, "I don't understand. What's going on? This is all very strange, Chuck. Who are they? And what do they want with *us*?" Chuck grunted, unsure how to answer and wrapped his tail around Nell to support her in the unsteady net.

On the ground, James and Hank had just managed to make

it back to the fork in the forest path after hearing the previous commotion. They both gasped, mouth and beak open, as they saw the five dragons flying away with the princess and James' dragon dangling precariously beneath them. Hank started fluttering around and squeaking in a frenzy whilst James kicked the ground in frustration. "Damn it, Hank!" he shouted. They both stared up, watching the other half of their travelling party getting further and further away.

Nell was semi-conscious as she saw the forests change to lakes and then mountains beneath her. Then, it all faded into darkness.

12. The Boss

As Princess Nell opened her eyes, she peered blearily at her surroundings. Her eyes widened as she realised she was no longer in the forest but somewhere else entirely. "Chuck," she murmured, "w...where are we?" Nell propped herself up on her elbow so that she could take a good look at the new place they had been taken to. She was shocked by what she saw. They were sat in the middle of a large plateau, extremely high up. The looming shadows of the mountains which surrounded the area were drenched in an eerie, fire-red glow from the afternoon sun and the silhouettes of dragons were swooping across the sky. She then turned her back to the mountainous view and focused on the other inhabitants of the plateau. Towards the far edge were dozens of large cages. At least half of these prisons were filled with five or six dragons each, of all shapes, colours and sizes which were roaring and whining in distress and despair.

Horrified by what she saw and heard, Nell instinctively looked above her towards Chuck and found him curled around her protectively. She sighed. At least she had *someone* to help her. In that moment, Nell grew curious and looked down. She gasped as she realised that they were, in fact, still trapped in the net and hanging from a huge, solid, wooden bar. The net didn't quite reach the floor. "Oh!" she exclaimed. Chuck snorted in agreement at the discomfort of the situation. Further along the plateau, to the left-hand side, sat a deep, blood red, canvas tent and a large, billowing bonfire with emerald green flames. On the other side of the unnatural bonfire, there stood an enormous, deep grey iron cage. It seemed to have a weird icy glow surrounding it. A tall, dark haired man was standing imposingly by the fire with his back to the princess and Chuck. He was shouting angrily at the four dragons that had carried the net from the forest and ordering them to bring him a plethora of unusual ingredients. Once they had flown off to complete their various tasks, he began throwing objects into the otherworldly fire in a majestic manner. "I wonder what he's doing," whispered Nell as green sparks flew out of the bonfire and a plume of black smoke began to billow upwards in a perfectly straight line.

Nell had been so distracted watching the sinister, almost magical man by the fire that she hadn't noticed the two, huge, intimidating oafs of men standing beneath the net. Suddenly, the scarlet dragon, who had battled Chuck in the forest, sped above their heads and tore down the net in which they were hanging with its teeth. They fell to the ground with a *thump* and it was only then that Nell looked up, stunned, to find the two ogre-like men towering over them with alarming smiles spread across their faces. This was *not* good. Before Chuck had the chance to resist, the men had wrapped a string of heavy, metal chains around his neck and wings. "That'll stop him from flying off, Kain" laughed the taller of the two.
"I can't wait to see what the boss has planned for him, Viktor," the slightly shorter but more menacing one nodded in agreement with a sly smile still spread across his face. The pair of them dragged Chuck, who was still too exhausted to fight back, across the powdery dirt of the plateau to the cage by the bonfire. They attached the chains, which were wrapped around the dragon, securely to the bars of the cage and left him in front of 'the boss' whilst they strolled back over to get Princess Nell.

Thoughts raced through Nell's mind as they approached. She should try to escape, but she didn't have a clue where she was. What's more, there was no way she'd be able to outrun them in the state she was in. Sighing, Nell resigned herself to her fate for now and braced herself for what was to come. "Look, Viktor," Kain chuckled to his brother, "I think she's scared.

Viktor laughed with an edge as sharp as a knife's blade; enough to unsettle even the strongest of characters and replied, "Do you think? It seems a shame to hand her over to the boss. She's such a pretty thing." As he spoke those last five words, he glanced over at Nell with threatening eyes. She quickly looked at the dirt, unwilling to meet his stare. Kain, the shorter, scarier looking one, scuffed his feet to a stop in front of Nell. "Up you get, miss," he ordered gruffly.

"That's *princess* to you," Nell grumbled as Kain hauled her to her feet by the shoulder, "and I'll teach you for laughing at me."

Once her feet were steady, the princess used all her weight and strength to headbutt the giant square in the nose. Her forehead made a connection, hard. Kain reeled backwards in pain and surprise, hands reaching for his nose. Blood trickled down towards his mouth and over his thumb which rested beneath. When he saw the blood he yelled, "ARGH! You broke it! Why you little..." Kain lunged for Nell wildly but she ducked under his flailing arms and began to run away towards the exit of the plateau.

"Wow," she muttered to herself, "my forehead's stronger than I thought!" A small smile played at the corner of her mouth as she ran, hearing the chaos behind her. Viktor sprinted over to Kain.

"Brother!" he cried, "Are you alright? What has that brat done to you?" Kain was still flailing one arm wildly whilst the other he held underneath his nose, catching the blood. He responded with a muffled bunch of noises. "What was that?" asked Viktor, puzzled. Taking his hand from his nose, Kain shouted, "The girl...*princess*! She's getting away!" Viktor snapped his head to where his fellow giant was pointing and saw that he was right. As he watched, Nell was dashing towards the mountain path at the back of the plateau. She was, however, quite badly hurt. This would be easy, he decided.

"Just... a little... further," Nell puffed as she tried to motivate herself in her escape. She hadn't planned this and knew it wasn't likely to happen but if she could just get off the open space of the plateau, she might stand a chance. Just then, she felt a crushing force from behind, knocking the air from her lungs. As she rolled in agony on the floor, she saw Viktor hovering over her with the same menacing smile on his face. "Did you really think you could outrun us, girl?" he baited, "You don't mess with me *or* my brother. You'll pay for your actions, but first, you're going to see the boss." Nell looked up at him and spat in his face violently. Viktor wiped the spit off his cheek with the rough cotton of his sleeve and bent down to pull the princess to her feet. "You'll pay for that, too, you little..." Viktor raised his hand and balled it into a fist.
"Viktor," a smooth, silky, intimidating voice interrupted from across the plateau.
"Y-yes boss?" Viktor stammered, shrinking into himself.
"I'm growing a little impatient and have no time for your personal vendettas. Bring the girl to me," the voice continued.
"Yes, sir, of course," he stuttered.

Viktor lifted Nell up with one hand by her dress and carried her carelessly over to the bonfire before throwing her forcefully to the dusty ground beside her dragon companion. He huffed and grumbled quietly to himself, glancing back at the princess, as he ambled off to tend to his brother's broken nose. Nell watched the self-centred oaf indignantly as he sauntered away. She shook her head. Now was not the time to be distracted by an infuriating idiot. The princess turned her attention to the figure by the fire. As she did so, another large human, though not as terrifying as the brothers, approached her with a glowing golden rope. He seemed to take great pleasure in binding Nell's wrists tightly and knotting the rope to the cage next to Chuck's chains. The ogre turned to the dragon with a gap-toothed grin and said pointedly, "And don't even *think* about breathing fire on that rope. It won't do anything; it's charmed."

"Leave us, Ivan," came the silky voice from the man still stood as still as stone by the fire.

The henchman pottered off as the silhouetted figure slowly turned around to face the princess. His face looked otherworldly, illuminated by the green flames. His face was dark and twisted but surprisingly handsome. His black hair fell softly in curls around his chiselled features and a neat, short beard flecked with silver highlighted his jawline. He had a strong, straight nose and his ice blue eyes pierced Nell as if he saw right through her. They were strangely familiar but she couldn't think why. 'The boss' had a veiled look as he held his hands carefully by his sides and began chanting in a quiet, insistent tone. His attention turned to Chuck and strange, green tendrils started to emerge from the fire, wrapping themselves around the startled dragon. Chuck began to pace on the spot, unsettled but unaffected by whatever it was that was happening. Nell was becoming increasingly agitated. "Hey!" she yelled, "What do you think you're doing?" The magician snapped his head to face Nell. His penetrating, aquamarine eyes boring through into the very depths of her being. "Quiet, girl!" he said sharply. He turned his back on the princess once more and started chanting. The green swirls started to appear again.

"Who are you?" Nell interrupted, "What do you want with us?" She saw the man becoming irate but kept going until he responded., "You'll be sorry you kidnapped me. I have the forces of two kingdoms searching for me!" The gentleman glanced back over his shoulder, momentarily shocked.

"Two kingdoms..." he murmured, almost to himself, then shook his head and chuckled, "don't be silly, child. The two kingdoms will not work *together*. They hate each other!" An evil smile played across the dark-haired man's lips as he relished in this thought.

"Is that all you're going to say? Aren't you going to answer any of my questions? Who are you? What do you want with us? And to be honest, what, exactly, is your problem?" Nell pushed. She immediately regretted this as the intimidating figure turned his whole body to face her. She took in his appearance in full detail. His clothing appeared to be that of a noble but was extremely tattered and worn. The burgundy clothes were partly covered by a sweeping, shadowy, fur cloak. He must've been around six foot three and seemed strong in stature. She looked back up to his neatly bearded face. The face now framed a full, beaming, terrifying grin. Nell instinctively shrank back behind Chuck as the dragon stood over her protectively and grunted.

"My problem?" he laughed wickedly, "What's *my* problem?" Suddenly he stopped laughing and his face fell into a deathly serious expression. "I can tell you what *your* problem is child. You ask too many questions. Keep that up and it might get you killed," he threatened without a trace of a smile on his face.

"I..." Nell began.

"But," he interrupted, "since you ask, I will tell you – no *show* you just who I am. The story starts a long time ago, before I was even born."

The bonfire suddenly roared into life and began to spark. The smoke filled the plateau and all around, the world seemed to alter and change. Nell and Chuck huddled close together, unsure of what was happening.

When the smoke cleared, they were in a narrow, cobbled street looking into the window of a small, unassuming terraced house.

"My mother lived in a small house, not far from the tavern where she worked," the man explained.

At that moment, a young woman of around 20 opened the squeaky wooden door to the house, slipped through the doorway and walked hurriedly down the road. She had raven black hair, emerald green eyes and full, peach lips. She was quite petite and had thrown a thick woollen shawl around her shoulders. Nell and Chuck followed the woman as she trotted down the street through the rain towards a building with warm light shining from the windows and sounds of shouting and singing coming from inside.

Suddenly, the smoke billowed through the image and Nell and Chuck were left spluttering. It cleared, this time, to reveal the same woman in someone's house. Another woman talked to her as she held her hands over a child's injured arm. Nell's eyes opened wide as she saw the strange white light radiating from the first woman's fingers in small swirls and spirals. The cut slowly closed and, eventually, completely healed. The light faded and the mother of the child hugged the healer. "Everyone loved her. When she wasn't working, she was a healer. The whole kingdom used to ask her for help and advice. Magic was illegal back then – it still is now – but she used it only to help others." He said, tenderly. As the smoke filled the scene for the second time, he continued, "She was working one night when she met someone."

The smoke dissipated to reveal the healer working behind the bar, wearing a loose white blouse and a long, brown skirt. She had her dark raven hair scraped back into a bun and her face was completely fresh and bare. *As Nell and Chuck watched curiously, a tall, confident looking figure approached the bar. They could only see the back of him to begin with. He had short, chestnut brown hair and broad shoulders.* 'He looks like my Papa' Nell thought as her breath caught in her throat. *Though he in fact looked nothing like royalty as he wore a simple linen pullover shirt and loose brown trousers.* "Excuse me, miss," *the stranger said softly. The healer searched the bar for the owner of the voice and, when she found him amongst the crowd of revellers, she smiled softly.*

"I haven't seen you here before. Are you new to the kingdom?" *Nell heard her ask.*

"No," *replied the stranger,* "I've lived in this kingdom my whole life but I've never been to this part of town. I thought I'd see what it was like."

"And what's the verdict?" *asked the healer, her smile creasing the corners of her eyes.*

"I think I've found a hidden gem," *the stranger confirmed.*

The healer moved from behind the bar and led the chestnut-haired man to a table. Nell was finally able to see his face. He had a soft, brown beard, high cheekbones and startling blue eyes. 'He's not Papa,' Nell sighed in relief, 'but he does look a lot like him!'

"They talked all night until the early hours," the magician said, interrupting her thoughts, "my mother fell in love that night. Soon, they were meeting every few days."

Smoke flooded the bar and their surroundings changed once more. Within moments, they were back in the woman's house. Her and the man from the bar hugged and kissed. Nell noticed the seasons changing quickly outside the little cottage. Before long, the raven-haired woman had a small bump which grew bigger and bigger.

"Soon, my mother became pregnant," the man explained.

In the small front room of the house, the lady stood stroking her stomach when the man with the kind smile walked in. At that moment, however, there was no smile but a frown on his face. They argued, though Nell could not really work out what they were saying. It was as though the sounds was muffled. The man stormed past Nell and Chuck, frustrated and walked out of the house, slamming the door behind him. After a moment, Nell looked back at the woman to see her sitting at the table, sobbing into her hands.

For a while, the scene faded, leaving them all back at the plateau. "What happened?" Nell asked, concerned.

"He left her," the magician said gravely, "he abandoned her when she needed it most. My mother fell in love with the *king* of Sundragon – your grandfather – and he refused to help her!" Nell's mouth fell open as she registered what had just been said.

"My..." she began, but the sentence refused to leave her mouth. She couldn't even form the right words as her mind whirled, trying to understand.

"After my *father* left," continued the man as though Nell was no longer there, "my mother became more cynical. Some say she lost her mind. In reality, she was heartbroken." The haze began to seep back in and soon the world had altered once again. *They were back in the healer's house except it wasn't as warm and welcoming as before. Instead, they were greeted with the sight of her huddled over a fire of unusual, green flames. Her hair hung over her shoulders, full of knots and tangles and the gleam in her emerald eyes had faded.*

"My mother turned to dark magic and then she had me. I learned everything I could from her about the dark arts," he noted. *A small child wandered into the front room, distracting the woman from the flames. The love in her expression was clear to see and, as the child grew (as though* time had sped up) they saw her teach him how to control the magic she was using. They practised together and the boy grew more powerful each day. He had his mother's raven hair and complexion but his father's build and startling blue eyes. The haze filled the room as the scene changed. "One day, she told me about my father," the man sighed heavily. "I couldn't believe she'd never told me. I was the oldest child of the *king*, the rightful heir to the throne. That, that coward turned his back on me and my mother and went back to his wife without a second thought. I got so angry..."

The smoke dispersed to reveal the magician, now a young man, arguing with his mother. They shouted and screamed at each other before a storm began to grow in the house. "Lucian, please!" his mother cried. But Lucian didn't hear her. His rage became so great that he started to throw green lightning bolts around the room. She hid behind the furniture to protect herself, unwilling to use dark magic against her own son. Instead, she tried to summon a forcefield and was surrounded by a pale, white bubble. Unfortunately, her white magic was not as strong as it had been in the past and the bubble soon burst as more lightning struck the floor around her. In a fit of anger, Lucian punched the floor and let loose an almighty burst of electricity which lit up the entire, darkened room. Once the thunder had settled and his rage had calmed, Lucian looked over to where his mother had been crouching and saw her lying motionless on the floor. Tears streamed down the young man's face as he cradled his mother's lifeless body where she lay. He let out a cry of such anguish that Nell had to bite her lip to stop the tears that were pricking her eyes.

The smoke entered the house, bringing the princess, the dragon and Lucian back into the present. As Nell looked over at Lucian's face, she saw the same look of anguish as she had seen on the young man in the vision. He shook his head, as if returning to reality, and looked down at the ground. Balling his hands into fists, he hissed vengefully, "That *king* failed my mother. He failed me. I *will* sit on the throne of Sundragon. I will have my revenge!"

"And how, exactly, do you plan on doing that?" Nell asked, a little shell-shocked.

"Well, girl," Lucian replied, his eyes switching from pained to gleeful in a matter of seconds as he looked at the princess, "I'm glad you asked."

13. Panic

James paced up and down the same piece of path in front of the log in the forest for the sixty-second time in the space of three minutes. Hank hovered behind him in a fluster of flapping and squawking. The prince was wracking his brains as to what had just happened. Had he really seen Nell and Firestorm, his dragon, carried away by a team of *other* dragons in a net? "Hank," he stammered, "w...what just happened?" Hank chirped incessantly in James' ear. He was just as panicked as the prince. Neither of them knew what to do. There was another CRACK above them in the canopy of leaves. Both the prince and the hawk jumped at the sound, unsure what was going to happen. Hank flew under the collar of James' royal blue jacket to hide. "Alright, Hank," James soothed, "I'm sure it's nothing *too* terrifying." Prince James edged backwards, preparing himself for the worst whilst Hank tucked himself further under the collar.

The canopy rustled and heaved with whatever was above them. With another ear-splitting SNAP, the branches finally gave way and the creature came crashing onto the forest floor. James ducked behind the log, peeking out over the top to see what was happening. Underneath the mass of leaves and branches, he could see something moving slowly. Hank was still chirping loudly in James' ear. "Shh, Hank!" he whispered to the baby hawk, "It'll hear you." Hank stopped squawking quickly and just as he did, the creature suddenly stopped moving. James stood up tentatively and stared at the pile of foliage. "What do we do, Hank?" James hissed, "What if it's hurt?" Hank refused to come out from the prince's jacket and didn't make a sound. "You're right," James said resolutely though Hank had said nothing, "I *have* to go and see if it needs help." Much to Hank's horror, James stepped over the log and started walking towards the now extremely still creature underneath the leaves on the forest floor.

Upon reaching the pile, James crouched down before brushing aside some of the leaves and branches. His eyes widened as he saw the creature laying underneath. It was a lynx cat cub. The cub was still fuzzy with sandy brown fur, striking amber eyes and little black tufts at the tops of its large, pointed ears. Its paws were the size of James' hands. Hank started cheeping in a panic as, typically, lynx cats were carnivorous and *definitely* not friendly. The prince looked over the cub to check it for injuries and saw blood coming from its hind leg. The lynx cat was awake, but clearly not fully conscious. It was whimpering softly and yelped when James reached for its hind leg. "Sorry, little guy," he said softly, "I promise I'm trying to help." The cub's eyes were trusting and it blinked slowly, almost as if it understood. James continued to examine the leg, which was badly damaged and cut from the fall. He tore a small strip of cloth from the front of his shirt and wrapped it around the gashed leg in a makeshift bandage. Once it was knotted, he whispered, "There you go little one, all fixed up." The lynx stumbled to its feet and, purring, rubbed its head against James' hands. "Hey, Hank," James said, "I think we've got ourselves a friend and I *think* she's a girl. What shall we call you?" The prince thought for a moment, "I know, we'll call you Ilana, since you fell from the trees." The small cub gave a short growl. "I think she likes it," James said to Hank, cheerily. "Now," he continued, his expression sobering, "what shall we do about Firestorm and the Princess?"

14. The Plan

Lucian's eyes glistened as he finished telling Nell his plans, "And that's how I'll get my revenge, take the throne from your stupid father and regain my place as the rightful King of Sundragon."

"You, you, nasty piece of work!" yelled Nell, lunging forward towards Lucian aggressively. Lucian backed away, surprised and a little scared by her outburst. However, she was soon restrained by the rope attaching her to the giant cage and, no matter how she struggled, she couldn't break free. Lucian, who had quickly recomposed himself after Nell's sudden charge, began to laugh darkly. He walked right up to the princess until he was inches away from her face.

"I am nasty," he grinned spitefully in a low, rough voice, "and there's *nothing* you can do about it." The princess growled angrily and Chuck joined in with his teeth bared. Lucian ignored this and turned to the bonfire. "Now then," he announced, "where was I? Ah yes, of course." The magician's eyes misted over in a foreboding green fog as he started to chant in a low, humming tone.

Nell couldn't work out what he was saying but, as he spoke, terrifying, swirling tendrils slithered out of the bonfire and began to surround Chuck. The sky darkened to a stone grey and the princess was sure she heard thunder rumbling in the background as bolts of lightning lit up the newly storm-filled atmosphere. Chuck tried to bite the spirals but they disappeared into a vapour. He shook his head, feeling confused and a little disorientated. He span around, his eyes following all the different, twirling wisps of emerald green surrounding him. Lucian's chanting came to an end and he turned to face the dragon. Chuck glanced at Lucian, his head cocked to one side inquisitively. His eyes were wide and his mouth slightly upturned, unsure of why Lucian was staring at him. Was something supposed to happen?

The dragon looked over at his friend, Princess Nell, with the same quizzical look on his face and snorted. Nell looked just as puzzled as he was and simply shrugged in reply. Chuck plodded over and sat down with a soft 'thump' next to Nell. *'Well that was weird. I'm not sure what he was trying to do to me,"* Chuck's voice sounded in Nell's mind.
'I don't know either, Chuck, but it was definitely a little odd. You don't feel any different do you?' Nell thought back.
'Not at all. Maybe it didn't work, whatever it was," came the dragon's reply. Nell's mouth lifted at the corner in a small smile to reassure her dragon friend before turning her attention back to their captor. Lucian was pacing the ground around the bonfire so quickly that the dust was rising beneath his feet. He was muttering to himself, getting louder and louder until finally, "ARGH!" he yelled, "Why didn't it work?"
"Why didn't *what* work?" Nell questioned, feigning innocence.
"The spell, stupid girl!" he shouted, "The spell didn't work. But *why*? What did I miss? Was there something else I should have done?" The magician thought for a moment, staring into the abyss at the centre of the bonfire, the blaze reflecting creepily in his eyes. The green tendrils of fire spat upwards into the still clouded sky and sparks popped above his head. Finally, he stepped back from the flames and barked, "Viktor! Kain! Ivan! Where are you three idiots?"

From somewhere behind the princess, the two, still rather intimidating, brothers and the gap-toothed brute came running. "We're right here, boss," chirped the shorter one, Ivan. He still had a silly grin on his face; a grin which faded immediately when he saw his boss' expression.
"Well done, bird-brains," Kain jibed, "now you've made him angry."

"Yeah," joined in Viktor, "now we're *all* going to get it!" All three henchmen fell silent as Lucian turned to face them.

"Quiet!" he demanded, "Did it not occur to you that I can hear every word you say?" The oafs looked between each other, worried.

"N-no, sir. Sorry sir," Viktor stammered, barely able to get the words out of his mouth. He hung his head low and gazed hard at the floor.

"I'm working with a bunch of buffoons," Lucian sighed to himself, rolling his eyes.

"Pardon me, sir," Kain interjected. Both the men beside him stared at him in disbelief.

"What is it, Kain?" snapped Lucian.

"I couldn't help but notice that the dragon still seems, erm, normal. Is that intentional?" Kain questioned.

"That's it," raged the magician, "I've had enough of you three and your interfering! Ivan! Viktor!"

"Yes, sir?" both the brother and the gap-toothed ogre replied quickly, standing to attention.

"Leave now, before the sun sets and find me more dragons. My army isn't anywhere near large enough for what I have planned," Lucian ordered.

"B-but where will we find them?" Ivan stuttered, "We've already captured dragons from all areas of the mountains."

"I don't *care* where you find them you fool, just find them!" the boss bellowed. The two henchmen turned swiftly towards the back of the now shadowed plateau and hurried away to do as they had been asked.

Once they had disappeared from view, Lucian turned to Kain who was noticeably shaking with fear. "Now," smiled Lucian cruelly, "Kain."

"Y-yes boss?" Kain spluttered.

"Come here," Lucian whispered. As he did so, two startling green tendrils shot from the fire and wrapped themselves around Kain's waist and legs. Slowly, they pulled Kain, his heels dragging through the dirt, towards his boss. Kain's eyes filled with panic, unnerved by the magic surrounding him and by what awaited him when he eventually reached his master. As the seconds ticked by ever so sluggishly, Kain drew ever closer. Lucian glared at him through ice cold eyes, daring him to react or struggle. The tendrils unravelled and returned to the fire as, at last, Kain stood in front of the magician. His knees were trembling. He was petrified. He raised his eyes apprehensively to look at the tall, grim figure before him. Upon meeting the smug, frozen eyes glimmering with triumph, he immediately returned his gaze to the ground at his feet. Lucian raised an arm and a clap of thunder rumbled in the sky. Kain quivered and held his breath.

"Think you can do my job better than me do you, fool?" Lucian sneered.
"No sir, not at all sir," Kain replied, the words spilling out of his mouth like a raging river.
"Well you seemed to think so earlier. Go on, *you* try connecting with the dragon," Lucian urged.
"What?" Kain was beginning to panic.
"You heard me. Stand by the dragon and connect with its mind, try to control it" Lucian taunted.
"So *that's* what you were trying to do!" interrupted the princess. Lucian winced when he heard her voice. Why was she always getting in his way? *She* didn't seem to have any problems getting close to that ridiculous dragon. Suddenly, a thought struck him. His entire face lit up so much that Kain instinctively backed away from the magician and Chuck curled himself round Nell protectively.
"Don't worry, Kain," Lucian smiled, "I'm done with you. I've got a better idea."

"Oh?" Kain replied, relieved.

"Lock those two up in the cage they're tied to. I've suddenly become extremely interested in the bond they seem to share," Lucian trailed off as if in deep thought and Kain instantly threw the princess in the cage. He did this with great satisfaction, remembering the pain from his nose earlier. Hesitantly he approached the dragon who growled at him uncomfortably. Grabbing a stick from nearby, Kain prodded and nudged Chuck into the cage with Nell. Once they were both inside, Kain sighed and slammed the door shut, locking it with an enormous bolt.

"You're not getting out of there any time soon," he chuckled to himself and turned to leave.

"Oh, and Kain," Lucian called to him. Kain froze and anxiously waited for his master to finish his sentence. "Next time, *don't* question my methods, do I make myself clear?"

"Of course, boss. I'm sorry, I won't do something so stupid again," Kain mumbled and quickly hurried away to the other side of the plateau.

When Lucian had lost sight of Kain, he swivelled on one heel to assess the pair in the prison he had made for them. "I wonder," he thought aloud, "what can I do with you two. I'm sure I can come up with some way for you both to be useful to me, now that I can't control you, sun dragon. Maybe I'll just have to find out if I can control someone who *can*." Having finished his thought, Lucian turned back to the fire and, with a small swoop of his right hand, the flames fizzled into nothingness.

15. Going Home

As night fell, James, Hank and their new friend Ilana were still pacing beside the log. James walked in front, Hank hovered by his shoulder and Ilana the lynx cub limped behind, never quite making it to the end of the path before having to turn to catch up with the prince. They had been doing this for hours, trying to come up with a plan, a rescue strategy for Nell and Chuck the dragon. "I don't believe it," James sighed, "she actually does need saving this time and I'm stuck here, walking up and down with no clue what to do." Defeated, James flopped down on the log with a bump and rubbed his face with his hands, resting his elbows on his knees. Ilana padded over to the prince and reached her front paws up to his lap. She nuzzled his hand and began to purr loudly. A smile tugged at the James' lips as he stroked the big cat's forehead. Now a little calmer, Prince James began to think more clearly. "You know, Ilana, I think you're right," he decided aloud, "we need to go home."

Hank turned to James, confused and chirping. "No, Hank," James assured, "not your home, *my* home." Newly motivated, James sprung up from the log, collected Hank and popped him on his shoulder and ran down the path the way they had come that morning towards his own castle. Ilana ran along beside him without using her injured paw, easily keeping up. James' plan was simple. He would return to his castle, let his parents know that he was okay but needed to help a friend who was in danger because of him, take his weapons (sword and bow and arrow), his armour and leave again before they had the chance to stop him. Once he had got out of the castle, he decided that himself, Ilana and Hank would head to the mountains to save the princess and Firestorm from the dragons and whatever else might be up there by... well, the last part was a work in progress. He was sure that by the time they got to the mountain, they would have thought of some form of plan of action.

They made their way through the forest swiftly along the paths. James knew his way home from anywhere in the forest as he'd flown it so many times with his dragon whilst they had been hunting. This meant that finding their way back to his castle was a much easier task than that of finding the princess' own castle. This time, he knew exactly where he was going. The sun was now on its downward descent towards the horizon as the dusk approached. James, Hank and Ilana would need to hurry if they wanted to make it to the mountain before nightfall.

16. A Collision

Meanwhile, in the woodlands of the Kingdom of Sundragon beneath the setting sun, the King's Guard were trawling the forest for any signs of the missing princess. Lawrence, the Captain of the Guard, was leading the search through the undergrowth, leaving no area unsearched. Five other knights followed behind a little less enthusiastically and grumbled to each other along the way. "How does she always manage to get herself into so much trouble?" moaned one of the knights.

"Heaven knows," another replied, "but there's clearly enough trouble around since she seems to attract it wherever she goes."

A third guard chipped in, "And it's always us that have to clean up the mess afterwards." All the guards nodded and grunted in agreement,

"So, what *exactly* has she done this time?" the fourth, slightly more timid guard asked hesitantly.

"Well," the second knight began eagerly.

He was interrupted by a very irate Captain of the Guard, "That's enough!" Lawrence cut in, "*She* is the princess, boys so watch your mouths. Actually, it isn't her fault this time. Princess Elenore has been kidnapped by a rogue dragon. Reports from some of the villagers are that she fell somewhere near here. It's up to us to find out where the dragon has taken her."

The rest of the guards avoided meeting Lawrence's eyes, embarrassed at their behaviour and feeling somewhat awkward. "Right, all of you, back to it. We've got to keep looking until we find the princess," Lawrence urged. The knights returned to looking through the undergrowth with renewed enthusiasm and vigour, now determined to find Princess Nell before sundown. They checked under logs, bushes, leaves and even up trees but their search was fruitless. The group strayed further and further from the villages into the deeper woodland until they bumped into something manmade.

The knights lifted their eyes to find a large wooden sign which read, 'Welcome to the Kingdom of Skyrain'. They all stopped in their tracks and looked to Lawrence. "Well, Lawrence, I mean sir, what should we do?" one of the men asked.

"*Surely* you can't expect us to go in there?" another one gasped, eyes wide with worry.

"They'll have our heads!" the first knight cried. All the men began to panic, muttering under their breath and wailing to each other in fear of their own lives.

"Pull yourselves together!" Lawrence ordered, "We are the King's Guard for goodness' sakes. Look gentlemen, the Kingdom of Skyrain must understand the need to look for our princess. I am sure they are reasonable people." Most of the men seemed comforted by this thought but one knight was still unsure.

"What if *they* were the ones who took her?" he blurted. Lawrence was becoming more annoyed by the second.

"Have some sense, man! Why would they want to kidnap the princess? A dragon took her and the people of this kingdom can't control those creatures any more than we can. I've had enough of this. We're going into Skyrain!"

The knights all followed Lawrence's lead and gingerly tiptoed up to the sign. Carefully, they stepped over the imaginary line between the two kingdoms holding their breath. When nothing happened, they all exhaled in relief and returned to their search once again.

*

In a different part of the same forest, the King's Guard of the Kingdom of Skyrain were trudging through the vegetation. Benedict, the Captain of the Guard, led the search for the prince, who had been gone for longer than usual on his hunting trip. The guards were discussing their annoyance with the search. "Can you believe the queen?" asked one of the knights.

"I know," replied another, "why does she worry so much?"

"She's always got us out here chasing after James," a third knight interjected.

"The lad can look after himself; he's not a boy anymore," a fourth added.

The first guard responded, "That's not what *she* seems to think."

"Hey now!" interrupted Benedict protectively, "*she* is the Queen and she has every right to be worried right now. There are dragons flying over these forests and no one knows why they have left the mountains."

"James has Firestorm," the first knight replied dismissively, "why should we worry?"

Benedict let out a grim laugh, "Firestorm has never even *seen* another dragon before."

The other knights in the group started muttering to each other. Their panic began to rise until one of them blurted, "D-did you say dragons? Why are we here? We'll just be their next snack!" the rest of the guards began shouting and hurrying back the way they came towards the Castle of Skyrain.

"That's it," cried the third guard, "I'm out of here!" As they turned to run, Benedict blocked their path. The guards piled up behind each other, all trying to push and shove their way past the Captain.

"Soldiers!" bellowed Benedict. Then more softly, he continued, "We are the King's Guard. We are brave. We do not run and we do *not* moan about our duties. James is out here somewhere and he could be in trouble. We are the best of the best so let's find him!"

The soldiers hung their heads, ashamed of their actions and looked stiffly at the floor. One of the knights looked towards Benedict and asked, "How long do you think we will be out here?"

"As long as it takes to find the prince. So, the quicker we can find him, the quicker we can go home," replied Benedict.

"Yes sir," the guard mumbled and carried on with the search. The group searched more thoroughly as they moved through the forest, overturning leaves and logs and looking in bushes and hollow trees as they went. Without realising it, they were walking closer and closer to the border with their neighbouring kingdom.

Suddenly one of the groups backed into something solid. "Ahh!" he yelped. All the knights looked around to find themselves face to face with the King's Guard of Sundragon. The knights from both kingdoms immediately raised their swords, ready to defend themselves. Benedict was equally as shocked as his colleagues but managed to demand answers.

"Knights of Sundragon, why are you here?" he asked.

Lawrence, who was also stunned replied, "Lower your weapons; then we'll talk. Both sides looked at the other, unsure whether to lower their weapons first. Eventually, both Captains lowered their own weapons and the knights followed.

"Now," Benedict breathed with relief, "what brings you to Skyrain?"

17. Trouble

Heading towards the castle of Skyrain, James, Hank and Ilana were beginning to run out of energy. Ilana was now limping more obviously on her injured paw and Hank had settled on James' shoulder as he was too tired to fly. They were flagging and desperately needed to sit down and recoup. James spotted the trunk of a long since fallen tree and slowed to a stop beside it. "Come on, Ilana," he called softly, "let's rest a while. We'll not make it back if we carry on like this." James stretched his legs out in front of him and gazed at the horizon where the sun was starting to disappear beneath the trees. As he looked towards the mountains, he scrunched his nose as he wondered where the princess and his dragon friend, Firestorm, could be. He thought about what had happened and hoped with all his might that he would be able to save them both. He couldn't help but feel that all of this was his fault. The dragons circled the mountain, small and seemingly harmless. All except one. That one appeared much larger than the others. In fact, much *closer* too. James' eyes widened and he instinctively ducked behind a nearby tree, taking Ilana with him, as he realised that the dragon was heading straight for them.

The dragon moved at incredible speed as it barrelled through the trees to land with a *thud* where the prince and his companions had just been sitting. The dragon sniffed the air loudly, trying to pick up on their scent. All too soon, its head snapped to the large tree behind which James, Ilana and Hank were crouched. "I think it's time to move," whispered James, grabbing the two animals beside him. Without a second to spare, James sprinted out from the wide trunk and dashed across the path to another large tree just as the flames from the dragon's mouth engulfed the bark of their original hiding place. Slightly breathless from the run, James panted, "We're going to need a plan. This isn't going to work for very long." Realising that the lynx cub and baby hawk were unlikely to talk back to him in any form of normal conversation, James decided this task was his alone. He looked around him for anything he could use as a weapon and his eyes rested on a large, straight, pointed branch in the middle of the path. It would be a risk to move into an open space but one that was necessary if they wanted to survive more for longer than the next ten minutes. He would have to strike the dragon quickly before it had the chance to react and burn him to a crisp.

James timed his jump to perfection. He threw a small stone by a tree further from the path, away from Ilana and Hank. Once the dragon had gone to investigate the strange noise, he rolled into the middle of the dirt path and scooped up the spear-like stick with one hand. He ran up behind the dragon and lunged with the branch, piercing the dragon's scales on its leg. The dragon yelped in surprise, a sound which was soon followed by an angry cry as it turned around to see James standing resolutely, brandishing his makeshift spear in the clearing between the undergrowth. "Come on then, you brute," challenged James, "come and get me!" James locked eyes with the dragon, daring it to attack. The dragon did not disappoint. With an almighty roar, it charged towards the prince and reared its head, preparing to throw a fireball in his direction. This was the moment James had been waiting for and, whilst he dragon's neck was exposed, he threw his spear with all his strength at the creature. The branch became lodged in the scales between the dragon's chest and shoulder joint and the animal cried out in pain. James winced as he didn't enjoy causing others pain, especially not dragons. But this was self-defense.

The dragon began to faulter but was still slowly advancing on the prince. Suddenly, Ilana sprung out from her hiding place and pounced on the dragon's tail, biting down hard. With another squeal of pain, the creature began to flap its wings, deeming the potential meal not worth the hassle. As it took off, it threw Ilana to the forest floor with a large swish of its tail and flew quickly back towards the mountain. Prince James sank into the floor as relief and exhaustion washed over him. That was too close. This clarified the reason he needed to head back to his castle before trying to save Firestorm and the princess; he could never take on the number of dragons in the mountains without a weapon.

Then, as he looked for his companions, he saw one of them sprawled on the floor, "Ilana!" he cried, running to her side. The lynx cub had taken a nasty knock when she was hurled to the ground by the fleeing dragon, which had rendered her unconscious. James picked her up tenderly and set off along the path once more. "Come on, Hank!" he called, "We've got no time to lose! We've got to save Firestorm and Princess Fleur, and Ilana needs some care at my castle before we head out again." Hank hurried over to the prince and hovered at his side as they continued to make their way through the forest, both shaken by what had just happened. James peered over at the setting sun. They really had better hurry; night was falling fast now.

18. Discovery

Beneath the twinkling sky of dusk, in the middle of the forest at the borderline between the two kingdoms, the captains of each guard were in a heated discussion. "So, tell me," Benedict demanded, "why are you in the Kingdom of Skyrain?" The knights of Skyrain glared at the men from the other kingdom accusingly. There was an obvious sense of hatred behind their eyes.

"Our princess," Lawrence replied, matter-of-factly. Benedict looked puzzled.

"What do you mean, your princess?" he quizzed.

Lawrence shrugged and answered, "She's missing."

"Missing?" Benedict gasped. The other guards mumbled in surprise.

"Yes, a dragon flew off with her a couple of days ago and our intel suggests she has been dropped somewhere in this area," Lawrence informed the Skyrain captain.

"Oh, I see. That's terrible news," muttered Benedict.

Lawrence turned to his own group of knights, who were stood awkwardly, unsure of what to do. He spun back to face Benedict, determined not to be the only one interrogated. He needed to save face in front of his men. "And why has Skyrain sent out what looks like a search party?" he pushed. It was Benedict's turn to feel uncomfortable at parting with information.

He studied the ground intently for a few minutes before sighing and replying, "We're looking for the prince." A small smirk formed on Lawrence's face when he realised that both parties were out with the same aim.

"The prince?" he encouraged, wanting to hear more.

Benedict sighed again, "The Queen is worried because he has spent longer than usual out on his hunt – she's a little over-protective. Due to the dragons in the area, she asked us to come out and ensure his safety but there's no sign of him so far." Realisation dawned on Lawrence, the captain of Sundragon's army.

"So, he's missing too?" he asked Benedict.

Benedict frowned, contemplating the question, "I suppose you could say so, yes." After it was established that both royals were missing, the knights from both kingdoms whispered amongst themselves with shock and worry.

Lawrence looked towards the sky, seeing that the clouds and darkness were drawing in. "Perhaps we should all report back to our kings that both heirs are missing. This could be more serious than we thought," he suggested.

Benedict's brow furrowed as he considered before responding, "Perhaps you're right. Night is falling so we would be unlikely to find them now anyway." The captains turned to their men.

"Right men, we must head back to the castle to inform the king. Move out!" ordered Lawrence.

"You heard him," Benedict called to his soldiers, "we should return to our castle. Let's go!"

*

When the King's Guard returned to the Kingdom of Sundragon, Lawrence was ushered quickly into the Great Hall where King Robert was waiting for him. He looked up expectantly as the Captain of the Guard entered the room through the large, impressive archway. "Well?" asked the king. Lawrence looked at the floor, debating how best to tell the information he has learned to the ruler.

"Unfortunately, your majesty, the princess could not be recovered," he said, regretfully.

"I had thought as much," King Robert sighed, a little deflated.

"Though I *did* gain some information, your highness," Lawrence continued.

"Oh?" prompted the king.

Lawrence took a deep breath before starting his recount, "Our search for the princess took us into Skyrain territory in the forest." He paused as he heard a sharp intake of breath from King Robert. After a moment, he returned to his story, "We ran into Skyrain's King's Guard whilst we were in their kingdom. They were out searching for their prince."

"Their prince?" interrupted the king.

"Yes sir, something about a hunting trip. They were uneasy because dragons have been seen over the forest and they don't usually leave the mountains," Lawrence confirmed.

"They're uneasy about dragons? How unusual," pondered King Robert, "of course, *we* are, especially now my poor little Nell has been taken. She must be so frightened all on her own."

The king sat on a nearby chair next to the grand dining table, rubbing his face with his palms. He would never forgive himself for letting her out of the castle that evening. He should have held her back or been quicker to react when she ran out into the gardens. Lawrence saw the king's anguish and walked over to sit beside him, gently placing his hand on his majesty's shoulder. This would have usually been frowned upon but King Robert and Lawrence had long been good friends. "Sir, if I may ask," Lawrence began tentatively. The king looked up sharply as the captain's voice broke through his thoughts.

"Yes, Lawrence," he responded kindly, "what is it?"

Lawrence cleared his throat before asking what he knew was a bold question, "Why *do* we dislike dragons so much? Or, perhaps, why do they dislike us?" At this question, a hazy mist clouded the king's eyes as he settled into his chair. He gazed out of the window wistfully, remembering his family's and his kingdom's history.

"We didn't always hate each other, you know," he started.

"Sir?" Lawrence encouraged.

"-the Kingdom of Sundragon and dragons. There was a time many years ago when dragons lived with the people of Sundragon in harmony," he continued.

"So, the legends are true!" murmured the captain.

"Indeed they are. Humans and dragons worked together to build this kingdom and the dragons formed a close bond with the townsfolk. Dragons and humans living together. It's not something we could imagine now," sighed King Robert, "The royal bloodline had an incredibly strong bond with one dragon family in particular – the kind that gave our kingdom its name – the sun dragon. It is said that the dragons and royals shared a bond so strong that they could communicate without speaking and hear each other's thoughts. The sun dragons became the protectors of the royal family. Their connection with our family helped them to reach adulthood and, in return, the dragons protected us and gave us their trust. The bond between dragon and rider was unbreakable."

"So, what happened?" Lawrence asked, engrossed in the story. The king's face changed, it became contorted and pained as he recalled the words passed down by his ancestors.

"One day, everything changed," he stated, "When my grandfather's father became king, he did not hold the dragons in the same regard as previous kings. He saw them as possessions, something that could bring him financial gains. He treated the dragons terribly and planned to use them as weapons of power against other kingdoms." King Robert's eyes flashed with anger at the thought of the actions of his great grandfather. He resumed, "There came a time when the dragons could take no more. They fought back and, whilst they were reluctant to hurt the townspeople, many were killed in their following battle for freedom. Even the most loyal dragons left eventually or they would not have survived, including the sun dragons. They fled to the mountains where they have remained ever since. "

The king rose from his chair and walked to the window, his gaze lingering at the peaks on the horizon line. "Thanks to my great-grandfather, the dragons never returned," he sighed, "They will not come near the kingdom as many of the dragons who escaped will still be alive today and remember what happened the last time they were here. The townsfolk are terrified of dragons now as the stories of the burning kingdom are told everywhere." He turned away from the window, eyes still slightly misty and looked at Lawrence honestly, "So you see, it was a shock to see the dragons here in the gardens the other day and now they have the princess... my daughter." His voice broke as King Robert finished his sentence, a sob catching in his throat. Lawrence held the king's gaze confidently.

"Your highness, I never knew the full story. We *will* find her – the princess I mean. But if the Prince of Skyrain is also missing, is it possible that they are lost together?" the captain asked. Upon hearing this, the king's demeanour changed. He stood up tall and puffed out his chest as if feeling threatened. "Together?" he growled, "No, that won't do. That's not acceptable."

"Sir.." started Lawrence, sounding uncertain.

King Robert walked up to the captain until he was an inch from his face. "You must go back out, Lawrence," he ordered, "and search the entire kingdom again. We must find her. Whatever you do, do *not* cross over the border. Take your men and leave."

"But sir," Lawrence stuttered.

"At once!" shouted the king.

"Of course, your majesty," Lawrence nodded, puzzled, "We will leave at once."

The Captain of the Guard turned and strode out of the Great

Hall, heading to regather his soldiers and return to the forest. The king watched him leave and then collapsed, defeated, back into his chair. "Lost with the Prince of Skyrain," he muttered to himself, "Oh my little Nell, what *have* you got yourself into?"

*

In the other kingdom, Benedict and his knights returned to the castle of Skyrain. As soon as they walked through the gates, the captain was hurried through into the Grand Ballroom where King Alfred was waiting rather impatiently. "What news, Benedict?" he whispered anxiously. His wife, Queen Minerva was sat at the other end of the hall by the great dining table, wringing her hands with worry.

"Ah, your majesty, I'm afraid we couldn't find Prince James," Benedict replied.

"Oh? I wonder where he could be then," the king muttered to himself.

"But we did come across something rather interesting," Benedict continued lowering his voice. He looked over at the queen, knowing that if she heard what he was about to say, she would become even more hysterical so he moved closer to the king. "We bumped into the King's Guard of Sundragon near the borderline in the forest, your highness." King Alfred raised his eyebrows in surprise, "Sundragon?"

"Yes, your majesty. They were looking for their princess. She was taken by a *dragon*," Benedict whispered.

"That's worrying. It's bad enough that the dragons are out of the mountains but for them to venture into *Sundragon*. Something isn't right, Benedict. I don't know what, but I can feel it in my bones," the king said ominously.

King Alfred sat on a small lounge seat next to the large, rectangular window and sighed desperately. He knew that the queen was right; this was a worrying time. Benedict approached the king softly and crouched next to him to meet his eye level. "Your majesty," he asked curiously, "why don't we associate with the Kingdom of Sundragon? They are, surely, our most likely ally."

The king looked at Benedict, assessing the intent of his question. When he found it to be pure, he began his tale, "It was a time long before my own, Benedict. There *was* a time when the two kingdoms were allies. It was a wonderful time – or so I am told. The dragons thrived and worked with the people of Sundragon. The kings were friends. All seemed well." King Alfred paused a moment as he imagined what it must have been like. "However, all that changed suddenly when Edward became the king of Sundragon," he said grimly.

"Who was King Edward?" asked Benedict.

"He was the current king's great-grandfather. Edward was a cruel and unfair ruler. He had no respect for the dragons and used them for his own gain. As a kingdom blessed by the heavens, Skyrain could not condone his actions and, when my great-grandfather found out that Edward planned to use the dragons to attack our people, he cut all ties with the king," finished King Alfred.

Benedict looked at the king in awe. He had knelt down on the floor whilst the king was telling the story and only now began to stand up. Before he was fully upright, the captain asked one more question, "That was a long time ago, my king. Why are we still at odds now?"

King Alfred's eyes saddened, "The alliance was in tatters and the dragons left Sundragon at the same time as Skyrain severed ties. Neither kingdom has ever tried to rebuild the friendship, though it has been some time since the events I've told you. I'm afraid we're all too stubborn. I cannot be seen as weak by trying to mend old wounds. Honestly, it would take a miracle to bring the two kingdoms back together."

From across the ballroom, Queen Minerva spoke to her husband in a voice which was barely audible, "Alfred, dear, with James and Sundragon's princess both being lost at the same time, you don't think?" The king turned to his wife, his face turning red with anger at such a thought.

"You're right!" Alfred shouted, "They could be lost together! That's completely unacceptable. We must find James at once! Benedict?"

"Yes, your highness?" the captain said nervously.

"Go back into the forests and take your men. You must find the prince swiftly and whatever you do, do *not* cross the border. Do you understand?" commanded the king. Benedict knew the chances of finding the prince in the dark were slim but he also knew better than to question the king.

"Of course, your majesty, we will set off immediately," he replied and rushed out of the ballroom to gather his guards.

As Benedict left, Queen Minerva approached Alfred. She stood him up and wrapped her arms around him, pulling him into a close embrace. They stayed like this for a long time as tears trickled down the queen's cheeks. Alfred simply held her and said nothing – what was there to say?

19. The Return

James, Hank and Ilana had been walking for what felt like an eternity. James was sure they should have been back at his castle by now but had to keep reminding himself that they had travelled for nearly two days in the opposite direction with the princess. The path was well worn in this part and surrounded by large hills. They trudged forwards, knowing that they must reach their destination as quickly as possible – the lives of their friends were at stake. The path was extremely familiar to James now. It was one he had ridden many times when he and Firestorm were out hunting. They would be back at the castle within an hour. As James walked, he let his thoughts drift to his best friend, his dragon. They had known each other since they were both infants. The prince was just twelve when he met Firestorm. They needed one another. He shook his head and brought himself back to the present. There was no way James was going to let anything happen to his best friend *or* the princess. He scrunched up his face in determination and quickened his pace. "Come on, you two," he called to the hawk and the lynx, "we'll be there in less than an hour if we hurry!"

As they continued towards the castle, the path began to get bumpier. There was mud all over the road as well as branches, roots and large boulders. James frowned with confusion and worry. The walkway wasn't usually like this; this wasn't a good sign. He looked around him and saw that the hills beside the road were caved in. They looked as though a giant had taken large chunks out of them with enormous hands. His eyes widened as he saw trees on their sides, half-way into the holes which had clearly been pulled from their original homes in the soil. This could only mean one thing. At that exact moment, the earth began to quiver. James rushed to Ilana and scooped her up, placing her around his neck. He dashed as fast as his tired legs could manage over the rocky, shuddering path, dodging the roots and branches as he ran. He made his way out of the hill-lined area but didn't stop there. The prince kept running and didn't look back even though he could hear the thunderous cacophony of mud and rocks crashing to the ground. He continued until the rumbles of falling rubble were a faint murmur in the background before slowing to a breathless stop. James slipped Ilana gently onto the floor before collapsing, exhausted next to her on the dusty ground. "That was terrifying," he admitted to the baby hawk, who was still hovering above them, and the lynx lying beside him, "let's not do that again any time soon!"

After a long while sprawled out on the floor, Prince James scrambled to his feet and began walking again, though a little more cautiously than before. "Right, Ilana and Hank, we need to get moving if we want to have any hope of reaching my castle before the end of the night," he said, trying to motivate himself as much as the others. All three of them set off again, more determined than ever to reach the end of the pathway, to get out of the forest and to save their friends.

*

King Alfred and Queen Minerva had moved from the grand ballroom to the entrance hall of the castle, anxious to hear any news the guards brought back immediately. They had no intention of sleeping until they knew their son was safe. The queen rested her head on her husband's shoulder and sighed, "How long will we have to wait, Alfred? My heart breaks every second longer he is gone." The king placed his hands gently on her shoulders and looked her in the eyes, lovingly.

"We will wait, my love, as long as it takes," he replied, his tone warm and soothing, "we should hear back soon now, they can't be too far from finding him." Minerva scrunched her nose as she considered the alternative.

"But what if..." she began.

"Shh," interrupted Alfred, "we shouldn't think of what ifs yet. We don't need to. Captain Benedict will find him." The queen buried her face in King Alfred's collar, unable to speak for fear of the tears she held in escaping her body.

Their heads snapped to the door as they heard a sudden rattling. The rattling grew louder until, with an almighty shove, James burst through the huge, arched doorway and entered the hall, followed by a small hawk and a wild lynx. His parents rushed towards him as the prince tried to get past them to prepare to rescue his friends. "James!" cried his mother, "Where on *Earth* have you been? We've been worried sick."

"Do you know how many people are searching for you right now?" questioned his father in a mixture between relief and anger. Both of his parents were trapping him, fussing over him and getting in his way. James was surprised that his short absence had caused such a disruption but he was determined to carry on as planned. "Excuse me mother and father," he said quietly, "I just need to get through." The prince pushed through the two royals and sped off towards the castle's armoury, closely followed by Hank and Ilana.

The king and queen stared unbelievingly at the wild cat. "What is *that*?" screeched the queen. King Alfred sighed, knowing that James couldn't help befriending wild animals. After all, that's exactly what had happened with Firestorm.

Prince James returned from the armoury wearing a protective, leather tunic and carrying a deadly looking sword. He had a quiver filled with iron-tipped arrows and a lethal bow slung over his shoulder. His parents stared at him blankly. "Why are you dressed like that?" asked his mother.

"Please don't worry, mother, but I need to go back out," he replied.

"OUT?" she shrieked. James winced at the high pitch of the queen's voice.

"What your mother means," King Alfred interrupted, slightly more rationally, "is why do you need to go out again? You've been gone for days and there are dragons roaming the forests. You're not safe out there, son." James placed the quiver gently on the floor as he assessed the situation with the king and queen. He needed to be honest with them to be allowed back outside. Well, mostly.

"I know what you think, mother, father," he began, "but I have to go back out there. Firestorm has been taken and the pr... Fleur – this girl I met whilst I was hunting – she's been taken too. I have to find them. I can't just leave them when it's all my fault," James stopped himself before he divulged too much information.

King Alfred stammered, "F-Firestorm is *gone?*"

Queen Minerva was more bothered about the other piece of information James had shared, "Who's Fleur, James?"

"Why are you bothered about the girl?" King Alfred asked the queen in an accusatory manner. James had already stopped listening to the pair of them and, whilst they started arguing, was rifling through his satchel to ensure he had packed enough food for the journey. He then strode past his quarrelling parents and headed back out of the enormous, castle doors. As the tail of the lynx swished out of view, the king and queen realised that their son had already left. They called after him but they soon understood that it was too late. James had gone once again.

James ran along the path to the gates of the castle. He charged through them with his two animal companions and hastily set off on his way to the mountains. The sun had set now and the darkness of night had fallen. Somewhere in the distance, an owl hooted and the wind blew an eerie chill across the kingdom and the forest beyond. The prince knew they were in for a challenging night.

20. Camp

The sky glowed a rosy red over the mountains as the sun peeked above the horizon. Its light cast an eerie shadow over the camp on the plateau as the bars from the cages in which the many dragons were held were mirrored on the dusty ground. The camp lay beneath several tall mountain peaks which were surrounded by a thin layer of mist making them seem almost mystical in the early morning sun. Nell and Chuck rubbed their eyes sleepily, huddled together after an uncomfortable, cold night in their cage. They were rudely awakened by brothers Viktor and Kain noisily unbolting and hauling open the large, barred door in front of them. They stomped into the jail-like box with the princess and the dragon. Chuck growled at them ferociously and backed into a corner with Nell protected behind him. Viktor smiled wryly and untangled the dragon's chain from the metal bars. He yanked the links hard, digging into Chuck's neck. Although the dragon tried to resist, he was weak from exhaustion and lack of food. He didn't have the energy to put up much of a fight and soon submitted to being dragged out and leaving the princess behind on her own.

"Why does the boss always want the awkward ones?" grumbled Viktor, "He never goes for the nice, calm dragons that are happy to walk with us."
"At least we get to leave that little *wretch* behind for now," muttered Kain, glancing back over his shoulder at Princess Nell. She caught him looking her way and threw her weight forward threateningly whilst glaring at him. Her face was dirty and her dress was ripped in many places. Her hair was even more tangled than usual, giving her an almost tribal appearance. He turned around sharply and shuddered. She

was something else, he thought. She was *wild*. What Kain didn't see was that, once he had stopped staring at her, Nell had curled up into the fetal position in the corner of her cage, shut her eyes and imagined that she was somewhere else, anywhere but the plateau.

Viktor and Kain continued to tug Chuck all the way to the other side of the camp until they were in front of Lucian's personal tent. The tent itself was made of a luxurious navy-blue fabric and had a small, pointed roof. There were some strange symbols embroidered on the cloth doors to the small marquee, embellished with gold. They might have been symbols of dark magic. Viktor nervously approached the tent doors and coughed to clear his throat. Before he even had the chance to speak, he heard his master's voice, "Viktor, Kain, you idiots, I'm by the bonfire." They looked past the billowing tent to the edge of the plateau to see the twisted magician towering over the large, smoking bonfire (which had been moved away from the cage since the night before), dressed in a black, velvet, floor-length cloak inscribed with more symbols of golden thread. "Bring the dragon to me," Lucian commanded coolly. Viktor gulped and Kain ran his hands through his matted hair nervously. They'd already managed to annoy their master the night before and had no intention of doing the same again. Hurriedly, they heaved Chuck over to where the magician was standing. Chuck tried to dig his claws and heels into the ground but the dust was so thick that he could not seem to find an adequate place to grip. Instead, his feet simply slid along the dirt with little difficulty, much to his irritation. The dragon growled quietly in his throat, a low rumbling sound which made the hairs on the brothers' necks stand on end. Though he was drained, Chuck reasoned with himself that it would be sensible to try to either escape or return to Nell as quickly as he could. He started to build smoke and flames in the back of his mouth. As the fire became larger, the corners of his mouth began to glow.

In an instant, Lucian snapped his head to look at the dragon coming towards him. He uttered a short phrase in an unfamiliar language and Chuck was drenched with water, dousing the fireball he was trying to form. Shaking his head vigorously, Chuck the dragon snorted in disgust as his only plan of escape, quite literally, went up in smoke. Viktor and Kain finished pulling him to the desired position in front of the magician and wrapped his chain securely around a looped post protruding from the ground. The dragon relented and flopped down with a loud thump, plonking his head onto his tail like it was a pillow. He had no more energy left to fight. "Perfect," Lucian smirked, "Viktor, Kain, leave us." They both nodded curtly and retreated to the safety of their own tent at the other end of the plateau. Dark magic made them feel uneasy.

"Now then," Lucian began, turning to face the dragon at his feet, "let's see what we can do with you. We'll give this one more try." The magician's eyes glowed with a terrifying white luminescence as he started to chant in an ancient language. Smoky tendrils of various colours swathed the sun dragon as Lucian cast an array of different spells. Each one failed to affect Chuck. With growing frustration, the cruel man continued to cast spell after spell. As his anger increased, so did his casting speed. After just a few minutes, Lucian stopped – red faced and breathless – and yelled in exasperation towards the fading stars. Once he had vocalised his annoyance at the spells' failure, he composed himself until he was able to coolly examine the dragon in front of him. It appeared that the creature was entirely unaffected by his efforts and was staring at him, confused. The dragon kept looking between the magician and his cage. Lucian, unthinking, followed Chuck's gaze and glanced over at the cage. His eyes flashed with understanding as he caught sight of the princess curled up in the corner.

A devilish grin crept across his face. "Do you know something?" he asked the dragon, "You may have just given me an idea. I considered it last night and now I have a feeling it might work." Chuck shook his head, confused. This was the last thing he wanted.

With a single flick of his wrist, the wisps of dark magic had unlocked the cage, picked up the princess and carried her next to the spot where Lucian was standing. She landed on her feet, surprised and a little disoriented. *'What's he doing, Chuck? Are you okay?'* thought Nell.

'Don't worry about me," Chuck's voice replied in her mind, *"I'm fine. I'm more worried about why he has brought you over here. Stay close to me."* The princess shuffled closer to Chuck the dragon whilst keeping her eyes trained on Lucian. Both of the captives were on edge, unsure of the magician's next move. Lucian was now hunched over the bonfire, which made him seem less intimidating than when he stood at his full height. He was rummaging through the ashes, muttering in the ancient language as he searched. Suddenly, he stopped and raised aloft a strange looking artefact. It was long and pointed, almost like an elongated dagger. Upon the rounded blade was a crest of a Celtic sun. this was the same crest that could be seen on Chuck's forehead and the same design as the crest of Princess Nell's kingdom.

Lucian's chanting grew louder and he approached Nell. Chuck growled, baring his teeth in warning but the magician threw the dragon aside like he was nothing with a small wave of his hand. The princess tried fearfully to back away from him, but Lucian held her rooted to the spot with a single stare. His eyes bore straight through her head as though he could read her innermost thoughts. And yet Nell could not look away. When Lucian was close enough for the princess to see the hatred gleaming in his eyes, he took the blade and gripped it with his left hand. He dragged the edge across the palm of his hand, slicing the skin and causing a stream of blood to trickle from his closed fist to the floor. Nell's eyes widened as she saw this. He was a mad man. She needed to run but her feet would not move. Panic began to rise inside her as the magician reached her.

With a vengeful smile, Lucian gently lifted the princess' hand. She was powerless to stop him due to the dark magic swirling around her. She tried to ball her hand into a fist but the magician opened her fingers with ease. He took the artefact, drew the blade across her palm and muttered a phrase in the ancient, Gaelic tongue. She winced at the searing pain she felt in her hand as her blood dripped over her fingers. Then, Lucian did something very unexpected. He clasped his own bloodied hand to hers, gripping tightly. As he did so, he muttered 3 more words, "Ceangail sinn còmhla." His ice-cold eyes locked with hers and everything went black.

21. Memories

Unaware of the strange happenings on the plateau, James, Hank and Ilana had finally reached the edge of the forest at the bottom of the mountain range. They were dishevelled and fatigued from a full night of travelling. James' sandy, golden hair was untamed and ruffled whilst Hank's feathers and Ilana's fur were still covered in the dust and rubble from the previous day's disasters. James was deep in thought as they walked in silence and, without warning, started talking to Hank. "Hey, Hank," he said, looking up at the infant bird of prey. Hank squeaked to indicate that he was listening. James continued, "I feel like we may have got off to a bad start. Well, I mean, I think *I* may have made a bad impression when Firestorm and I first met you and the princess in the forest." James paused at this point and looked to Hank for approval, understanding or some signal that he understood. Hank chirped as if to say *'Yes, you sure did make a terrible impression.'*

"I know, I'm sorry, you're right it was worse than bad," James sighed, "If I'm honest, I don't know what came over me. I've just spent the last few years of my life trying to live up to being a prince and I thought the best way to do that was to rescue someone. Only, she didn't need rescuing, did she?" James smiled half-heartedly at the memory of the princess' reaction to his bold claims of rescue. Hank squeaked apologetically, also remembering Nell's stubborn response to the interjections of the prince.

James remembered bitterly, "Only, now she really does need saving. Her *and* Firestorm both need our help. I want you to know that we will manage it. We'll get them back. I promise." James turned from Hank to the path in front of him and found himself directly at the bottom of the looming mountain range. "Well Hank, Ilana, it looks like we're here," he gulped. The mountains created an imposing shadow as their impressive height blocked out parts of the sun and sky. Dark clouds circled the tips of the peaks and the silhouettes of dragons could be seen swooping and gliding amongst the haze. James looked meaningfully at Hank and Ilana. The hawk and lynx were clearly shaken by the near impossible task and yet they were still by his side, ready to try. James was moved and coughed surreptitiously to clear a threatening lump in his throat. He mumbled to them both, "Thank you for this; for being here and not leaving." Then, summoning all his courage, in a more convincing tone he said, "Let's do this."

*

On the plateau, Chuck and the princess were back in their cage. Chuck was curled around Nell protectively and nuzzled gently on her lap. Nell sat motionless, staring at the bonfire which still flickered with those enchanted, viper green flames. They danced in her pupils, almost entrancing. Chuck had tried to talk to her after she had woken up. He knew Lucian had cut her but the dragon didn't understand why she had shut him out. She had put up barriers around her mind and would not let him in. This unsettled the dragon. It was like she was afraid of something. He shuffled closer to her. Nell held her injured hand carefully. She had wrapped a makeshift bandage around it using the bottom of her dress when she first woke up. Now, however, she couldn't think straight. Her mind felt heavy, as though she wasn't in control of her own thoughts. This scared her. Chuck had tried to speak to her but she didn't want to let him in. She didn't know what was going on in her own mind so how could she expect the dragon to understand it? He might not be safe there.

Instead, she focused on the flames. They were beautiful,

almost hypnotising. They were enough to distract her from the fog in her brain and the uneasy feeling she was getting in the pit of her stomach. She didn't know what the words meant but she couldn't get what Lucian had said out of her head: *"Ceangail sinn còmhla."* It was like the phrase was playing on a loop. His voice was coming from all angles again and again. Nell scrunched her eyes closed and covered her ears with her hands. Why wouldn't it stop? *"Ceangail sinn còmhla. Ceangail sinn còmhla. Ceangail sinn còmhla."*

*

James, Ilana and Hank were now part way up the towering mountain. The rock face was steep and often sheer meaning that James had to climb as though scaling a cliff. Ilana was a skilled climber and Hank could fly, but for James, this was exhausting. He pulled himself up onto a more level surface as the mountain path started to even out. "Phew! Thank goodness for that," he panted, "I don't think I could take much more rock climbing right now." James lay on his back, breathing heavily. He needed a rest. "How much further do you reckon, Hank? We *must* be nearly there by now," he continued. Hank chirped doubtfully and flapped into the prince's vision, pointing his wings at the soaring highland above them. James chuckled, "Okay, okay, we still have a long way to go. But hey, a guy can hope!" As James lay sprawled out on the dusty floor, he felt vibrations under his body. "That can't be good," he muttered as the shaking became more pronounced. "No, no, not again!" he yelled, standing up and looking in the direction of the tremors. His fears were realised as he saw a flood of rocks, soil, trees and large boulders hurtling towards them. "LANDSLIDE!" shouted James.

He grabbed the two animals and dove for shelter beneath a slight lip in the mountain shelf above. They pressed against the shelf as closely as they could, praying that it would be enough to shelter them from the onslaught of debris.

Once the barrage of dirt and rocks slowed, the small ledge was somewhat buried in the destruction. Hank had managed to flutter above the flurry in order to avoid being crushed but he now started to panic as he searched for the prince and Ilana. There was no sign of movement underneath the rubble and Hank's heartbeat was quickening by the second. He scanned the area by the shallow lip under which the pair had been sheltering and chirped as loudly as he could. There was no reply. He flew in closer to the ground to get a better look but all he could see were torn up roots and branches and an awful lot of mud. There was nothing visible to indicate that James and Ilana were even still there, never mind whether they were safe. Hank swivelled around as he heard a small rattling coming from somewhere underneath the rocks. Suddenly, a hand broke through the debris, followed by an arm and a shoulder. The hawk swooped over to the extended limb and grasped onto it using his clawed feet. He flapped and pulled with all his might, trying to help the rest of the body escape. After a few minutes of battling against the debris, James heaved himself out of the landslide, coughing and spluttering. After catching his breath, he reached back into the mud headfirst. Hank chirped in alarm and tried to claw him back up but was not strong enough.

A few moments later, James returned with an unconscious lynx cub in his arms. He pushed her out of the now-settled dirt before dragging himself back to the surface. "Is..." started James before his lungs constricted and he had to regain his composure, "is she alive?" Hank hovered over her and was audibly relieved to see the rise and fall of her chest. He chirped to Prince James, who crawled over to the little lynx. James breathed heavily and whispered thanks to whatever had kept them safe during the terrifying, thunderous chaos of the last hour. He himself had little more than a few bruises and scratches, and Ilana was alive and looked to be in no worse shape than before.

James scrambled to his feet, aware that the more time they wasted, the less time they would have to save Firestorm and the princess. He carefully picked up Ilana, the lynx cub, and placed her around his shoulders. That would be the easiest way to carry her whilst she was still unconscious. She needed the rest anyway. He turned to the hawk, who was still hovering just above him, "Come on Hank," he encouraged, "we'd better get going if we want to make it to the dragon's lair by nightfall."

*

Nell curled up tightly into an even smaller ball than before. She was confused and terrified. Her head had become so heavy and misty over the last hour that she had no idea what was real and what was a product of her imagination. The only thing that kept her from screaming was the comforting warmth of the golden dragon wrapped around her protectively. She still hadn't spoken to him. She couldn't; not when she didn't even know what was going on in her own head. The flickering flames of the bonfire had only served as a distraction for a miniscule time and now she had nothing to stop her mind from wandering. As she sat there, shaking in fear of what was happening to her, she heard a whisper. It sounded like it was coming from the bonfire. *"Bonded together,"* it hissed, *"bonded forever."* Nell shook her head and blinked purposefully and rapidly, trying to snap herself out of what felt like a dream. When she looked at the bonfire again, it seemed perfectly normal and the voice was gone. She turned to face the other direction and was just about to drift off to sleep from pure exhaustion, when she heard it again. *"The dragon,"* it seethed, *"use the dragon. You must destroy..."*

"Stop!" cried the princess, breaking into a sob, "Just stop!" Chuck lifted his head anxiously. This was the first time she had spoken in hours and she wasn't making any sense. Her guard was still up so he couldn't talk to her, but he knew something was wrong. He nudged her shoulder with his nose. The dragon didn't know whether to comfort her or try to break her out of whatever hallucination she seemed to be having. He nudged her again, a little harder this time. Nell sat bolt upright after the contact and turned her head slowly to look over her shoulder. Chuck snorted, his heart racing as he anticipated what he would see. Her face was tired, her hair more wild than usual and her eyes were filled with tears, but she still looked like Nell. "Chuck?" she whimpered. The dragon tilted his head and rested it on Nell's lap. He huffed softly, trying to encourage her to keep talking. "I'm scared, Chuck," she continued, "I don't know what's happening to me. I feel all wrong and I keep hearing things that aren't there." Chuck roared, as he knew she'd understand and he couldn't speak to her telepathically with her preventing it. "You're right, maybe I'm just exhausted. It has been a weird and long day. Perhaps I just need some rest." As if on cue, the princess yawned loudly and settled back against the dragon's side. She quickly fell into a disturbed, restless slumber of frightening dreams and stomach-twisting nightmares.

*

By the time James, Hank and Ilana reached the plateau, the sky was blanketed by the last depths of the night. The stars were glinting sleepily in the sky, ready to disappear for another day, and the moon reflected a cool beam down onto the mountain range. James had pressed himself against a small mound on the outskirts of the area and carefully peeped his head up to assess his surroundings. The prince inhaled sharply as he saw the horrifying scene before him.

There were dragons everywhere. Most of them seemed to be in distress. They were either chained to the ground by their necks or packed tightly in cages with no room to move. Some of them roared out in anguish but others had simply given up. There were other dragons with red eyes perched on the ridges around the plateau. *'They must be the lookouts,'* thought James. Luckily, they appeared to have settled down for the night.

As James continued to scan the area, his eyes fell on a cage which was larger than the rest of them on the far side of the plateau to his mound, next to a mystical bonfire with moss green flames. This cage only had two shadows inside. One was definitely a dragon but the other was much smaller. "That's them!" he muttered under his breath. His eyes had adjusted to the velvety darkness around them and he could see the captives more clearly in the light of the moon. The princess looked in terrible shape. She was clearly drained and exhausted but she was also badly bruised and her clothes were ripped and torn. Had it not been for her startling blue eyes and the fact that she sat with Firestorm, she would have been unrecognisable. James' eyes moved to Firestorm, his closest friend. There was something different about him. He was larger, his wings looked stronger and his face looked more mature. The crest on his forehead glimmered a steady burnt orange and his eyes were brighter than before. The prince shook his head in disbelief. They hadn't been apart that long; how had he grown so much?

Firestorm was an adult dragon now. Although James was shocked about the changes his dragon friend had undergone, his attention was pulled back to the strange fire close to the cage. Beside it, he noticed a figure who had not been there before. Due to the light of the bonfire, he could only see his outline but that silhouette dragged a memory unwillingly from James' mind. As he stared at the flames, his eyes started to haze over until he was back in the forest as a 12-year-old boy in the middle of his memory.

James was sat on the back of a midnight black stallion, riding alongside his father, King Alfred. The king slowed his horse to a stop and dismounted, taking the creature to a nearby stream to rehydrate. James carried on riding, enjoying his time speeding through the trees. "Don't go too far, son!" called his father, watching the young prince ride past.
"I won't dad!" James grinned in reply, though he knew that his version of too far was entirely different to his father's. Still, he knew that it was not wise to ride out of help's reach in these woods alone. As he rounded a bend in the path, James heard two voices ahead of him. He tightened the reigns on his horse and stopped, getting down from the stallion and landing softly on the ground. Prince James quietly padded across the forest floor in the direction from which the voices were coming. "Keep an eye on those two, they're feisty!" a gruff voice said.
"Yeah, that little one won't be any trouble," came a second, deep voice, "For a legendary dragon, he sure is a wimp!"
"Dragons?" James whispered to himself. He shook his head. There was no such thing as dragons.

Upon reaching a small group of trees, James realised he was approaching a clearing. Peering through the leaves, he saw two large dragons of jewelled teals and blues. They were trapped in a cage with their wings bound, roaring in pain. "They are real," James muttered under his breath in disbelief. His attention was then drawn to a much smaller creature, an infant of stunning golden scales with a Celtic sun emblazoned on its forehead. The tiny dragon was backed into a corner by a brutish man carrying a large rod, pulsing with what looked like a magical energy. The man was brandishing the rod in front of the dragon, threatening to hurt it.

James steeled himself, pursing his lips together and stomped into the clearing. "You there," he called. The two men turned to look at the speaker and let out a snort as they saw the small boy in front of them. "What do you think you're doing?" demanded the prince. The thugs looked from the boy to each other and back to the boy again.

"Is he serious?" one of the men asked the other. They exchanged a look and turned to face James fully with menacing grins on their faces.

"What do you want, little boy?" probed the other hoodlum.

"Don't you know who I am?" James questioned, "I am the prince of this kingdom so do as I say; let these dragons go!" The prince was impressed at how brave he sounded. His courage started to dissipate when he saw the greedy glint in the men's eyes and he stumbled backwards towards the trees. "Not so fast, little fella!" the first brute shouted. The men lunged at Prince James.

Thinking on his feet, the prince ducked and ran between their legs as they reached for him. He took his small, child-sized sword and swung it at the lock of the cage holding the adult dragons. As he ran past, he swung the door open, leaving the enormous dragons free to escape. The two large men turned to see where the boy had gone and their greedy expressions quickly changed to ones of fear. They shook their heads helplessly and grabbed their weapons from their belts. The dragons immediately descended on them, lashing their tails and scorching them with flames. As the pair of giants tried to fend off the furious dragons, Prince James crept to the edge of the clearing where the small, golden creature was curled up in a small ball, terrified. James crouched down beside the little dragon and started to whisper to it. "Hey, little guy," he soothed, "don't worry, I won't hurt you. I'm here to help." The tiny bundle turned its face to the prince and snorted. James hesitated. He couldn't leave this helpless being on the forest floor. "Do you know what?" he said, "You can come home with me." With that, James scooped up the petrified creature and carried him like a baby in his arms. They walked past the two brutes, who were still unsuccessfully trying to fend off the two irate dragons they had captured, and back through the trees to the prince's horse.

The king was impatiently waiting by the stallion. It was clear that he had already been searching for Prince James as his skin was flushed from panic and exertion. "Hello, father!" James smiled, completely oblivious to the worry he'd caused. "James!" chastised his father, "Don't you ever wander off like that again. You had me extremely..." The king's words faded out as he looked at James properly and his eyes fell upon the creature in his son's arms. The king's eyes grew wide with a mixture of surprise and fear. "...and where did you find that?" he asked cautiously. James looked down fondly at the small dragon in his arms and looked back at his father, smiling even more.

"I rescued him from some bad men," the prince explained proudly, "He was scared and alone so I said he could come home with us. Can he please, father?" James looked up with pleading eyes at King Alfred. The king sighed affectionately.

"You want to keep a dragon, James? Are you sure?" Alfred probed looking slightly perplexed, "The creature is nearly as big as you!"

"Oh, but please, father," James asked imploringly, "He needs help!"

At that moment, the two brutish men, who tried to hurt the dragons and James, sprinted from the clearing and past the king and prince with a look of terror in their eyes. Their faces were covered in ash and their clothes and hair were scorched and charred. They were limping as they ran and they cowered in horror as the two stunning aqua dragons took off into the skies with a mighty roar. One of the bullies threw himself on the floor, hoping to protect himself whilst the other one let out an incredibly high-pitched scream. The adult dragons heard the sound and zoned in on the ogres. They began to follow them in the air. The screaming man noticed this and, dragging his colleague behind him, he sprinted as fast as his body would move down the path and out of sight. James looked after them as they ran.

"Were those the bad men, James?" asked King Alfred, a smile tugging at the corners of his mouth.
"They were. I sure showed them, father!" James replied happily. Alfred sighed, defeated.
"I suppose we can keep him. He does seem to have taken a liking to you," the king noted. It was true. The small dragon had snuggled into James' arms and was nuzzling his face into the prince's shoulder. He looked much more relaxed than when James had found him.
"Thank you!" James squeaked, overcome with joy. King Alfred lifted James and, with much effort, the baby dragon onto James' horse. Alfred did not mount his own horse but, instead, stayed on the ground to guide the two horses home safely. The king looked up at his son fondly, considering what a kind and thoughtful being he was becoming.
"What will you call him?" he asked. James looked puzzled and then frowned as if thinking extremely hard. Alfred laughed internally as he decided if the prince thought any harder he might burst.
After a moment, James replied with certainty, "Firestorm."
"Alright," the king smiled, "welcome to the family, Firestorm."

As James smiled, he noticed a bird in his vision. The bird would not move and was squawking in his face. Suddenly, the prince returned to the present, where they were hiding behind a large mound, scouting the area. "Sorry, Hank,"

James mumbled, "I lost my train of thought for a moment there." Prince James shook his head to wake himself up from his daydream. He glanced back over at the bonfire only to find that the mysterious figure had vanished. The prince inhaled deeply and returned to the task at hand. "Okay," he said to Hank and Ilana, "do we have a plan?" He looked at both of them expectantly and then muttered to himself, "Why would a bird and a big cat have a plan? James, you idiot." The lynx cub and hawk stared at James as he talked to himself, heads cocked to one side and unsure if he was going mad or just needed a minute. James turned back to them both and sighed with an impish grin, "Typical, the one day I have to fight through a mountain full of dragons and I only have you two for back up!" Ilana and Hank growled and huffed in protest at his cheeky remark. "I know, I know," he continued, "I'm only joking. Now, we need a plan."

22. Rescue

An hour later, a plan of action had been decided. James carefully skirted around the edges of the camp, keeping to the shadows and creeping from rock to rock. He intended to use this method to get as close to Firestorm and the princess' cage as possible before stealthily running over and setting them free. He wasn't sure how well guarded the plateau was or what other potential threats they might face. So, for now, James was on high alert. As James, Ilana and Hank made their way between two large boulders, they saw Viktor (one of the vicious brothers) heading their way on his rounds of the perimeter. They dashed for the rock ahead and scuffled to get behind it. Once they were there, Hank started squeaking to James nervously. "Shh, Hank," James whispered, "he'll hear you." The prince realised that it was already too late as he heard the thump, thump, thump of approaching footsteps on the other side of the stone. James made a split-second decision; they couldn't draw attention to themselves. As quickly and as quietly as he could, the prince jumped to his feet, stuffed his fist into Viktor's mouth and hit him deftly on the temple with the handle of his sword. The henchman was rendered immediately unconscious and crumpled to the floor.

The prince heaved a sigh of relief and whispered to his two companions, "Come on, quickly, before anyone else spots us!" The trio went back to edging around the camp, tiptoeing from boulder to boulder and somehow avoided the gaze of the four or five red-eyed dragons balanced on various precipices. More than once, James had to dash for the next rock for fear of being seen again. That couldn't happen if he were to save Firestorm and the princess. They kept creeping slowly closer and closer to the enormous cage which housed his friends. It felt like the small expanse took hours to cross.

Finally, they approached the cage.

Hiding behind the nearest boulder, James quietly called out, "Princess Fleur, Firestorm, over here!" The dragon's ears twitched as they picked up the sound from nearby. He swivelled his head in the direction of the sound, not quite believing what they heard. James peeked his head out from behind the rock and whispered, "Firestorm, I'm here buddy." Though exhausted, Chuck's eyes lit up with delight when he saw the prince crouching so close to him. The dragon snorted happily and nudged Nell with his nose to share the excitement. Nell turned around slowly, drained from her time on the mountain. She lifted her eyes from the ground to follow Chuck's eyeline in the darkness. Her eyes flickered with recognition as she started to see James' silhouette in front of her.

"Charming, you came," she murmured. Nell tried to stand to go and greet him at the bars of the cage but stumbled and landed heavily on her knees. She winced in pain but didn't make a sound save for a sharp intake of breath. Not thinking, James rushed to the cage and reached through the bars to help her. "Woah, Princess, hold on. I'll get you out just wait a second," he reassured her. The prince turned on his heel to face the lock of the cage. He unsheathed his sword and swung forcefully. The lock split with a clinking noise and fell to the ground. Prince James quickly unhooked the door and pulled it open with great effort. He assessed the restraints wrapped around Nell and Chuck and made quick work of the chains with his sword.

Nell was still in a heap on the floor, too weak to move. Prince James crouched over her tenderly and whispered, "I'm going to pick you up now, princess, so we can get out of here. I'm sorry, I know you don't need rescuing." James gathered her up in his arms and, as he was about to take a step towards his dragon friend, Nell raised her head and locked eyes with him. James froze to the spot, transfixed by her striking, aquamarine eyes and found himself noticing just how beautiful she was, even if she looked wilder than ever.

"Charming?" she whispered. He held her gaze until she lowered her eyes, feeling flustered.

"Yes, princess?" he asked, hopefully.

"Thank you," she replied. And, as if all her energy had evaporated, she leant her head on his chest and slipped into a state of unconsciousness.

"Firestorm," James asked, heading towards the dragon, "do you think you can fly?" Chuck looked at the prince with an excited glint in his eye. He was fatigued but extremely pleased at the suggestion that he could stretch his wings. He grunted a positive response at James and the prince understood. "Okay, that's good. Can you take us home, Firestorm? I think we all need to rest." Chuck shuffled carefully out of the cage and into the open, unfolding his wings appreciatively. Ilana clambered onto the dragon's back and Hank fluttered to perch on his head. James climbed up skilfully, still carrying Nell in his arms. With a few large flaps of his wings, Chuck took off safely and in no time they were soaring over the trees and fields. Soon enough, the shadow of the castle of Skyrain appeared on the skyline and Chuck increased his speed now that home was in sight. During the flight, Nell said nothing, remaining unconscious, and continued to lean against James. He could feel her soft breaths against his neck as she slept. The prince smiled as he glanced down at her fondly. He didn't want to wake her, so remained silent as they drew nearer to his home.

*

Lingering in the shadows of the plateau in the mountains, a pair of cold, ice blue eyes pierced the darkness. They had seen everything; the prince, the rescue, the escape, all of it.

As he considered the events of the evening, Lucian smiled, his teeth glinting menacingly in the moonlight. "How perfect," he murmured wickedly, "thank you for your help, *Charming.*"

23. Arrival

Silently, the dragon and his passengers swooped into the castle gardens in the Kingdom of Skyrain. As the party landed, the guards rushed inside to tell the king and queen their son had returned. James was tentatively dismounting Chuck, with the princess still in his arms, when his parents practically sprinted through the doors into the cold, night air. Ilana scrambled down from her resting spot and sat beside the prince, purring. His mother and father's eyes widened as they saw he was not alone. "W-what is that? You never did explain before," demanded King Alfred, pointing at Ilana. James looked down at the creature by his side and grinned.

"That is Ilana," he beamed.

"You *named* it?" the king replied incredulously.

"Yes, father, she is a lynx cub. We found her in the forest when she made a rather dramatic tumble from a tree. She hurt her paw on the way down and I couldn't just leave her there. She's very friendly!" And, as if to prove a point, Ilana purred even louder and rubbed her forehead against James' leg. "See," he smiled. King Alfred sighed inwardly and rolled his eyes. His son could never leave a creature in trouble; he always had to help. Their castle had become a zoo over the years with the various animals James had adopted.

The queen was focused on something entirely different. Her gaze was trained directly on the princess, who was still unconscious in James' arms. However, Minerva didn't see a princess, in fact, she saw something rather odd. It seemed the girl currently in the prince's embrace was feral, wild and entirely unkempt. She was covered in mud and her auburn hair stuck out at all angles, coated in dust. Her dress was stained and torn and, quite honestly, she looked a mess. "Never mind the cub," she quivered, "who is *she*?"

James looked at his mother softly and said, "This, mother, is Fleur, the girl I told you I needed to help."

"You never said she was a *wildling!*" Queen Minerva wailed.

"Actually," James said warily, "I may not have told you the whole truth earlier."

The king, who had been welcoming Chuck back to the castle with a good scratch behind the ear, returned to the conversation. "What do you mean, son?" he quizzed.

"Ah, well," James began, "she's not just a girl. And she's not a wildling either, before you say it again, mother. She's a princess."

"A *princess?*" both his parents chorused together. They looked her over again, disbelieving.

"Yes, she's a princess. She's been through a lot. Her and Firestorm were taken by a gang of dragons. We found them in the mountains, chained and caged, so I hope you don't judge by her current appearance." James looked tenderly at the sleeping woman in his arms and it was clear to his parents that he didn't think she looked a state at all.

"Princess *Fleur*, you say James?" his mother said, interrupting his thoughts. James shook his head and looked up abruptly.

"Yes, mother. Fleur," he replied. His mother looked thoughtful and placed a finger on her lips.

"I've never heard of a princess called Fleur before and I know every royal family for at least five kingdoms in any direction," the queen prodded suspiciously, "are you sure she is as she says?" James glared at his mother. He couldn't believe she would doubt him, though he still wasn't telling her the whole truth.

"Yes, I am sure. I trust her," he confirmed with a curt nod.

Prince James angled towards his father. "You must let her stay," he stated, "she needs to rest and I don't know where her kingdom is." King Alfred opened his mouth to protest but before he could, James had already started carrying Nell past his parents and up the exquisite marble staircase towards the guest bedrooms. He opened the door to the nearest one and went inside with Hank following close behind. James carefully laid the princess down on the bed and pulled the sheets and blankets over her body to keep her warm. She needed to wash and eat, but for now he wanted to let her sleep. She looked so fragile and peaceful lying in the bed. He couldn't believe she was the same girl who confronted him about his botched rescue attempt just a few days ago. James gently stroked her cheek before leaving and pulling the door to. He shouted goodnight to his parents prior to heading to his own room to recover. He would need his energy tomorrow so that he could get the princess home. For now, he would give in to the soft pillows and comfortable bed and enter the realm of dreams.

The king and queen still stood, shocked, in the hall. They watched as James took the girl to the guest room and emerged a few moments later only shouting a half-hearted goodnight before making for his own bedroom. Alfred and Minerva exchanged worried looks. "Minerva, love," King Alfred said, barely above a whisper, "you don't think that's the missing princess from Sundragon, do you?" The queen's face blanched as she considered this possibility.

"But, Alfred, the princess of Sundragon is called Elenore. James said this girl was called Fleur. That can't be the case," she decided,

"I know, but with their princess missing and a princess arriving at our doors with our son – don't you think that's too much of a coincidence?" the king continued.

"I must say, she does look very much like Robert and Lydia..." Minerva started. The queen shook her head, bemused. The child couldn't be from the Kingdom of Sundragon or she would surely have told James right away. What an absurd idea.

King Alfred realised that the dragon and lynx cub were still stood just outside the doors to the gardens. He called a servant, "Could you take Firestorm and *Ilana* to the stables to rest, please?" he requested politely. The servant bowed and led the two shattered creatures to their beds for the night. Once they were out of sight, the king looked at his wife, who was still deep in thought. "Minerva," he interrupted.

"Yes, dear?" she said, a little irate.

"I've never known him to act like that before, James I mean. Do you think there's something wrong with him?" he asked, perplexed and slightly anxious.

The queen smiled, "No, darling, there's nothing wrong with him."

"Then what is it?" the king persisted, "because something's different. That's not the James I know."

"I'm afraid he's in love," Minerva replied sadly.

"James? In love? With whom?" King Alfred started.

"I think you already know," the queen suggested.

"No, that girl? But they've only just met," her husband protested.

"I know," she soothed.

"And what if that *is* the missing princess of Sundragon? That would never do! My son cannot be in love with the princess of *that* kingdom! I forbid it!" the king raged.

The queen turned to fully face her husband and placed a comforting hand on his chest. She, in her mind, agreed that this was not an ideal situation. If the child really was heir to the Sundragon throne then they would have to try to extinguish the buds of romance well before they were recognised by the pair themselves. However, she also knew that it was no use trying to control her son's feelings. "I'm sorry, my love," she said to the king, "but there's not a lot we can do to stop it. If we're lucky, it will be a simple infatuation and once she returns to her own kingdom, things will go back to normal."

"And if not?" said King Alfred.

"Then we will have to take matters into our own hands. I won't have my son marrying some limpet he found in the forest," the queen replied venomously.

24. Gone

Light from the warm glow of the morning sun filtered through the curtains in Prince James' room. Small slithers of brightness shone on his face causing him to stir from his slumber. James sat up suddenly, his eyes wide. "Princess," he whispered in horror. In his dream, the princess had disappeared in the middle of the night and taken Firestorm with her. It had been so very vivid that James needed to check if it was real. The prince threw himself out of bed in his soft, tartan pyjama bottoms and rushed to the guest room in which Nell was staying. Once outside, he knocked urgently on the door. "Princess Fleur," he said, on edge, "Princess Fleur, please open the door." James knocked again and received no response. He swung open the door to find an empty bed, neatly made and no princess in sight. Only Hank, the baby hawk, was roosting on top of the large, embellished mirror on the dressing table. "Hank!" James shouted. The hawk jumped awake, nearly falling of his perch in fright. He chirped crossly at the prince but his squawking turned to panic when he also realised that his princess had disappeared. "Where did she go? Didn't you see her leave?" Not giving the hawk time to respond, James shoved some shoes onto his bare feet. If the princess was gone, what if his dream were in fact reality? He had to be sure.

Prince James burst into the stables to find an empty pile of straw where his dragon slept last night. The horses and Ilana were still there, but not Firestorm. "No! My- my dream... they're gone!" James yelled. Wasting no time, the prince sprinted back inside the castle and up to his parents' quarters. He forcefully pushed open the doors and ran into their room. "They're gone!" he cried. The king and queen were groggy from sleep and more than a little surprised to see their son in their bedroom.

"What do you mean, James? Who's gone?" King Alfred asked, not yet fully awake.

"Princess Fleur, Firestorm, they're both gone," the prince huffed, defeated and panicked.

"What on Earth, how are they gone?" questioned the queen, "They can't have just vanished!"

James took a step back and frowned. He had expected his parents to value his words, not question everything he said. He took a deep breath and tried again, "They're not here. The princess and Firestorm have gone. I have searched the castle and the stables and they are nowhere to be found." King Alfred and Queen Minerva started to take their son more seriously now he had explained. They got out of bed and went to stand by him to work out exactly what had happened.

"Hush, my child," Minerva soothed, "we'll find them. Are they not in the gardens on this fine morning?"

"No one is in the gardens, mother. I checked on my way back from the stables," the prince replied, becoming agitated. He needed to act fast. "Mother, I know the princess can't have been feeling herself when she left because her pet hawk, Hank is still in the room where she slept. She would never normally go anywhere without him," James said.

"A *hawk*?" his mother repeated.

"There's no time for this!" James snapped, "She could be in trouble. I don't need to remind you she was kidnapped by dragons. In fact, her whole kingdom could be in trouble. We have no idea what happened to her on that mountain!"

King Alfred, who had remained calm and controlled until this point began to show signs of worry. He put his hands on his wife's shoulders to calm her but his facial expression gave away his real feelings. "If that is the case, son, what will you have us do?" he asked James.

"Warn the kingdom. Warn her family. They must be told something is wrong!" James replied. The king looked bemused. He thought for a moment before he spoke again.

"But son," he said, "we don't even know which kingdom the girl is from. How shall we help them if we don't know who they are? You said yourself she never mentioned..."

James interrupted, "Father, I am afraid I haven't been entirely truthful with you and mother until now."

"Go on, James," Alfred prompted.

"You see, I know a little more about the princess than I first told you both," James confirmed.

*

Once they were fully dressed, the king, queen and their son hurried to the grand hallway ready to ride. Benedict, the captain of Skyrain's guard had brought round three horses. Two were those which belonged to the king and queen and the third was his own. Prince James had never needed a horse before with a dragon around. James looked up at Benedict, uncertain. "Benedict are you sure?" he stammered.

"Of course, your highness," Benedict replied, "this is an emergency and she is the fastest horse in the kingdom. I know you will be kind to her."

"Thank you, my friend," James said, nodding his head gratefully.

"Must we really travel there, Alfred?" Queen Minerva asked nervously.

"I'm afraid, my love, we don't really have a choice," the king replied soberly. The three horses and their riders galloped at high speed out of the castle gates and into the forest, hurtling towards their destination.

25. Ambush

The king and queen of Sundragon waited anxiously by the impressive, arched windows of the Great Hall. They had taken to waiting there in the mornings and for most of the day, hoping to finally see their precious daughter returning home. By now, however, they had almost given up hope of ever seeing her again. They searched the horizon for any possible clue which might lead to her return. King Robert took a step back as he saw a small, glinting shape moving on the skyline in the distance. He was puzzled. What could the shape be? "Lydia," he whispered, "do you see that glint over there?" The queen squinted and looked along the line of Robert's pointed hand to the golden fleck, which was barely visible over the forest.

"What is it?" Lydia gasped.

"I don't know. It's very unusual," the king replied. The pair continued to stare at the strange object as it got larger in the sky. Whatever it was, it was getting closer.

Lawrence, the Captain of the Guard rushed into the Great Hall. He looked dishevelled and was in a state of panic. He ran to the royals, spluttering and trying to find the right words to say. "Your majesties," he finally stammered.

"What is it, Lawrence?" asked Robert, anxiously. He had not often seen Lawrence in such a state. The captain was usually a composed, pillar of calm in any situation.

"The fields, your highness," Lawrence breathed, "the fields on the outskirts are ablaze!" The king's eyes widened with surprise and he averted his gaze back to the glinting object in the sky. Could that be the reason?

"Do we know the cause, Lawrence?" he asked. Lawrence paused for a moment, as if considering his response.

"We do, King Robert," he said. Robert looked at him impatiently, unsure as to why Lawrence hadn't explained already.

"Well then, man, out with it!" he snapped. Lawrence shifted uncomfortably on his feet; his eyes focused on a small fleck of dirt on the floor of the Great Hall. He gulped, preparing himself for the inevitable reaction to his response.

"Well," Lawrence said, barely above a whisper, "it's a dragon." Queen Lydia screamed.

"Just a dragon?" King Robert probed, sure there was more to the situation than his captain was letting on. Lawrence sighed. He had no choice but to tell the king and queen even though he knew they would not take the news well.

"No, your majesties," he began, "not just a dragon. The dragon is golden with the crest of a sun on its forehead – *our kingdom's* crest,"

"Oh!" cried the queen, looking as though she was about to faint.

"That's not all," Lawrence continued, "there is someone riding the dragon."

Once again, the king and queen's eyes were drawn back to the gleaming object in the sky. It was closer now and they could make out the shape of a dragon, its huge wings beating powerfully as it made its way towards the castle. Then, they noticed the silhouette of a petite girl with wild hair sitting astride the creature, unmoving. "No," muttered the king, "it can't be. She wouldn't."

"I'm afraid, your majesty, that Princess Elenore is the one riding the dragon," Lawrence admitted finally, hanging his head despondently.

"No!" cried the king, unable to contain his emotions, "not my Nell!" At that moment there was a huge commotion outside and the doors to the Great Hall burst open for the second time that morning. King Alfred, Queen Minerva, Prince James and Hank stumbled through the entrance, exhausted from a rapid journey to the kingdom and stood before the king and queen of Sundragon. King Robert turned, shocked, to face the unexpected guests. His surprise soon turned to anger as he recognised Skyrain's royal family. "How dare you," he hissed, "how *dare* you show your faces in my castle..."

"Robert, look," interrupted Queen Lydia, his wife, "it's Hank!" The king peered over at the other royals with some disdain, his eyes searching for the baby hawk. Lydia was not wrong. Hank was sat comfortably on James' shoulder and Robert's expression softened slightly as he realised that Hank clearly trusted the prince.

Noticing the king's hesitation, James stepped forward and began to speak, "Your majesties, I'm Prince James of Skyrain,"

"Please, say you know what's going on," pleaded Queen Lydia, "Why is our daughter doing this?" James saw the desperation in Queen Lydia's eyes and immediately empathised with her. the kingdom was being burned to the ground by its princess, her daughter; a fate no mother should have to bear.

"I found the princess a few days ago. I was out hunting in the forest with Firestorm, my dragon," James explained, "when we found her and Hank alone in the forest. She introduced herself to me as Princess Fleur, so I was unaware of which kingdom she came from, but I found out later that she was your daughter after I heard her speaking to Firestorm. We spent the following two days trying to get her back home but she was taken by five dragons and locked in a camp with a man involved with dark magic. Hank and I rescued her and Firestorm and brought them back to Skyrain to rest and recover, but they both disappeared during the night. When we awoke, they were gone."

Both royal couples gasped at this revelation; James had not

told his parents the whole story before, which meant that they were as new to this information as Robert and Lydia. King Robert squinted as he looked at James more closely. "Wait," King Robert said, "you look familiar, young man." James looked around sheepishly, not willing to meet the king's gaze.

"I don't see how, your highness," he replied.

"I recognise those eyes and your mop of hair. You're Sally's lad! You disappeared and broke my daughter's heart! How can you have the nerve to come here after all this time? And masquerading as a prince no less!"

"Robert!" chastised his wife, "You can't go around accusing other royals of being frauds!"

King Alfred of Skyrain stepped forward to explain, "Robert, he's my boy. There were some tragic happenings in his past but this boy is my son and quite clearly *not* the child you speak of, let's leave it at that." James looked at his father gratefully and tried to change the focus from himself back to the princess.

"King Robert, it's possible that this man has used his magic to control your daughter and my dragon. They formed a close friendship in their time together so he could be using that to his advantage," James said, "It's all my fault..."

"James," King Alfred soothed, putting a sympathetic hand on his son's shoulder.

"No, father, it is. We argued and I left her alone in the forest. Firestorm stayed with her but I left her vulnerable and unable to protect herself!" James lowered his head in shame, tears welling in his eyes.

"Sweetheart," his mother, Queen Minerva comforted, "you couldn't have known. This isn't your fault." James kept his gaze fixed on the flagstone floor, not wanting to speak again as he was uncertain he could make it through a sentence without his voice cracking.

"Prince James," King Robert said softly, causing James to look up a little, "whatever your past, you have done everything in your power to help my daughter. You couldn't have known that this would happen." James lifted his head fully, looking a little less guilt-ridden. He looked at both of Nell's parents.

"I am so sincerely sorry that I couldn't have done more," he whispered, still not trusting his own voice. The king and queen of Sundragon smiled at the prince for his kindness. Lydia's smile faded as her thoughts returned to the matter at hand.

"Robert, darling, why would this man want to hurt us, to hurt our child? We don't even know who he is," she asked her husband.

"Unfortunately, my love, I think I do," Robert replied grimly. He took a seat on the nearest chair and prepared to share the scandalous story with his wife and the other royal family. It wasn't something he wanted to do, but it was necessary for everyone to understand the situation.

The king cleared his throat before he began, "A long time ago, I found out that my father had an illegitimate son with a barmaid in the kingdom before I was born. The barmaid was a healer, a witch and, when my father chose to turn his back on her, she became obsessed with revenge. Her magic darkened and so did the son she was raising. Her son, my twisted half-brother, vowed to avenge his mother and I'm guessing this is how he's chosen to do it. I have to hand it to him, taking the kingdom and my child in one fell swoop, is quite the plan." He laughed darkly without an ounce of humour and focused back on the people in the room. They were all stood, mouths open, stunned into silence. Shaking herself out of her stupor, Queen Lydia of Sundragon cried, "Robert! Why have you never mentioned this?" Her husband looked at her pleadingly. Her expression softened and she changed her tact, "No matter, what can we do *now* to put a stop to all this?"

"Yes," added Queen Minerva, "she needs to be stopped before she destroys the whole kingdom."

"I – I don't know," Robert sighed. Both kings looked deflated and were unable to find a solution.

"Oh, for goodness sake!" Lydia scoffed, "I will go out there and stop her. She is my daughter after all and she'll listen to me, under a spell or not!" The two kings looked shocked at her outburst.

"Lydia, you can't!" cried King Robert, standing in protest.

"Why, do you have a better idea, my love?" the queen challenged. Robert sat again, backing down. He had nothing.

James stepped forward, "Excuse me, your majesties," he said quietly. They all stopped to listen to him. "If you don't mind, I'd like to go out there first. This is my fault; my responsibility and I should be the one to put it right." His parents looked at him anxiously.

"Must you go, James?" Minerva, his mother, asked.

"Yes, mother, I think I must," he replied resolutely. The prince turned to King Robert and bowed his head. "I will go out and retrieve your daughter. I fully intend to bring her back safely, with your permission," he said, seriously.

"Please don't hurt her," King Robert asked, his eyes pleading.

"I won't," replied James to the king and, as he walked away from his and Nell's parents, to himself he muttered, "I couldn't." James ran out of the Great Hall and through the castle doors, mounting the horse he had borrowed from Benedict. As he rode off towards the outskirts of the kingdom, both royal couples looked after him, distress and worry etched on their faces.

26. The Battle

James rode as quickly as he could. The kingdom itself was still standing and the houses were undamaged but people were panicked; rushing around trying to take cover and trying to find their loved ones, unsure of what would happen next. As he galloped further out into the fields, he started to see the devastation the princess and his dragon had caused. Crops and homesteads had been torched to the ground, leaving scorched, blackened dirt in their place. Small fires burned in patches where there was still some vegetation left. They were getting close now. The sound of blasting flames was getting closer and James could see their shadows up ahead. Once he reached them, James looked up and was taken back by what he saw. Nell's eyes were no longer their stunning ice blue but, instead, looked like two pieces of coal. Chuck the dragon's were just the same. The princess' hair swirled around her head in tendrils as if it were alive and the tips were glowing a strange, green colour. James couldn't believe what he was seeing. She was definitely not herself. This was going to be difficult. The prince took a deep breath and shouted, "Princess Fleur!" Upon hearing his voice, her head snapped to face him. Without a sound, Chuck turned to look at him too. They began to fly towards James, the dragon's wings pushing skilfully through the air. "Uh-oh," James muttered to himself, "time to move!"

Prince James nudged his horse and they sped over the blackened fields away from the princess and dragon. Without realising it, James had unwittingly brought the pair closer to the cobbled streets of the kingdom. He realised this too late as blazing hot flames rained down around him, setting fire to the rooves of the nearby houses. "No!" he cried as people were screaming and trying to find shelter. He veered away from the town and further out into the already burnt farmland, not wanting to cause any more damage. Nell and Chuck quickly caught up with him and aimed several balls of fire in his direction. Luckily, James was a skilled rider and managed to dodge the searing hot flames that flew past him, though many of them came too close for comfort. Finally, the prince slowed the horse to a stop in the centre of a charred meadow and waited, breathing heavily, for the princess to approach. "Okay, princess," he muttered under his breath, "let's do this."

The sun dragon took a deep breath in, preparing to let loose a blazing hot stream of flames. Nell glared at James with her soot black, soulless eyes and nodded to Chuck. James took this as his cue to move again and urged his horse to obey. He galloped left and right, dodging and weaving around the unrelenting river of fire. Suddenly, the prince remembered he had brought his own weapons. He reached behind him and swung his wooden bow off his back. With the other hand, he retrieved an arrow from his quiver and pulled it back ready to fire. He focused on Nell, knowing that the arrow couldn't pierce through Chuck's tough skin. Instinctively, the prince aimed for her chest but, just as he was about to release the arrow, he realised what he was doing. He couldn't harm the princess like that; he would never forgive himself. James adjusted his aim and instead trained the arrow on her right arm. He let go and it sailed into Nell's shoulder, piercing the skin sharply. James winced as it dug in. "Ah!" Nell cried in pain. As she was knocked sideways from the impact, the princess lost her balance and fell from her position astride the dragon. Chuck didn't realise until it was too late and she tumbled to the ground at great speed.

James galloped over on his horse and arrived, just in time, as she landed on the horses back in front of him, his arms cushioning her fall. James held Nell firmly with is hands, preventing her from getting away. She wriggled and struggled constantly, glaring at James angrily for keeping her there. As James tried to restrain her, he did not notice that Chuck had lowered his flight path and was hovering just behind him. As he was about to toast James with a ball of fire, Hank flew out from under James' coat. The little hawk distracted the dragon and engaged in a terrifying chase with him, looping and swerving across the sky, to allow James the time to talk to the princess. James held her tightly and forced her to look into his eyes. "Princess Fleur, this isn't you," he pleaded, carefully taking the arrow out of her shoulder as he spoke, "you are a kind, stubborn, fierce adventurer. You are a princess. Your mother and father are the king and queen of your kingdom, the kingdom you're now burning to the ground." Nell's gaze was not on James. In fact, she was still struggling with all her might to escape his grip. James held her more tightly. "Princess, it's not just your mother and father who need you, I-"

James' speech was rudely interrupted by the roar of an intimidating, scarlet dragon which had appeared nearby. The dragon hovered just above James and Nell and, as he looked up, the prince noticed a figure sitting on the dragon's back. His eyes flickered with recognition and he gasped as his memories returned to him. This was the man whose figure he had seen when he had rescued Firestorm as a child. This was the man whose figure he had noticed on the same dragon when the dragons had captured the princess and his Firestorm. This was the silhouette he had seen at the camp next to the bonfire from which he had rescued the princess. James hurtled back into the present and looked, furiously at the man before him. "You!" he shouted, angrily. Lucian looked down on the prince, applauding him sarcastically. "How touching, young prince. Who would have thought you'd be reunited with the childhood love you should have never met? Unfortunately, she'll never remember any of this.

Whilst her and your dragon were at my camp, I pushed them to their limits. They formed the unbreakable bond of the Sundragon bloodline and your dragon reached maturity," Lucian sneered.

James looked from Nell to Firestorm, confused. He peered back up at the menacing magician and asked, "But what has that got to do with *you?*"
"Idiot boy!" snapped Lucian, "This has everything to do with me. I'm the rightful heir to this kingdom but the girl's father, my wretched half-brother, took my crown from me. I raised an army of dragons to exact my revenge but I needed a particular creature to take the leading role." James turned desperately to Firestorm. "Yes," Lucian continued, "you took him from me once before, when you were young. Well I couldn't let that happen again. Though, I couldn't seem to control him like the other dragons. *That's* where your little princess came in." The horrid man smiled with malice at James as the prince started to understand what was going on.
"You mean," James started.
"Yes, that's exactly what I mean. That bond I was talking about," Lucian chuckled, "is the bond I'm exploiting to control your dragon. Robert has no idea what's coming for him. He will lose everything and his own daughter will take it from him!" Then, Lucian laughed; a deep thunderous sound which filled the skies with his hatred. "Princess!" he called.

Nell looked to Chuck, who immediately flew over without a word passing between them. As Chuck flew, he knocked Hank out of the air with a swish of his tail and was by Nell's side within moments. As she started to move, James gripped onto her arms tightly and looked steadily into her eyes, trying one more time to break whatever hold the magician had on her. "Princess listen to me. This isn't who are," he begged, "You're a good person with a pure heart. I know you're in there somewhere." He searched her face for some form of reaction but found none, so he continued, "You're the girl who refuses help when she is lost, the girl who is so stubborn it's infuriating, the girl who is so strong-minded she could never be a damsel in distress." Nell shook her head, unsettled and James noticed that her eyes flickered once between the coal black and her usual icy blue.

Lucian noticed this too, "Quickly princess!" he ordered, impatient to exact his revenge. The princess turned to leave once more but James held onto her arm and pulled her back to him again, refusing to give up. He sighed, he had to come clean about everything; who he was, how he really knew her, what she meant to him; all of it.

He pressed his forehead to hers and breathed, "I don't know if you'll ever remember this, but I know now what has been true all along. I can't lose you again. I need you, *Nell*, don't leave me like I left you." The prince took her chin in his hand and kissed her desperately. The princess blinked furiously, her eyes changing between soulless coal and striking blue as the inner battle raged inside her mind. Lucian frowned in concentration, trying to remain in control. He roared in rage as he lost his hold on Nell and her irises settled on their stunning aqua hue. Her eyes widened as she realised what was happening and she quickly pulled back, her cheeks flushing. James breathed in sharply as she pulled away but realised that Nell was no longer under Lucian's control.

"Uhm," he said sheepishly, rubbing the back of his neck, "it's probably best if you forget that ever happened, princess."

Nell shook her head, "You, you called me- but that must mean,"

Before she had the chance to piece her thoughts together, Lucian yelled, enraged, "How dare you destroy my life's work? You may think you have won this battle, but you still have to deal with me!" Without warning, an enormous blast of fire barrelled in their direction. They both cowered away from the sight, preparing themselves for the pain when it hit but it never came. As they looked up they saw Chuck, who was also himself again, shielding them from the blaze with his enormous wings.

"Chuck!" cried Nell, relieved.

"Firestorm!" shouted James, excited to see his dragon now he was free from the hold of the magician. Chuck snorted happily when he saw James but looked at Nell.

'Princess, you know what we must do,' the dragon's voice sounded in her head.

"You're right, Chuck," Nell replied aloud. The princess got off the horse and went to climb on Chuck but James caught her hand at the last moment.

"Let me go out there, princess," he begged, "I promised your father you wouldn't get hurt."

"You – you know who my father is?" she stumbled over her words. "No, never mind, you can explain all this later. I have to do this, Charming, This ones on me." Nell smiled as she let go of the prince's hand and climbed onto Chuck. "See you on the other side, Charming," she winked, then Chuck the dragon took off gracefully into the sky towards the blood red dragon and Lucian, determined to set things right.

Nell and Chuck cautiously approached the garnet red dragon and its rider, anticipating some form of instantaneous attack. They were right to do so as Chuck barely managed to dodge around a stream of intense flame which bellowed a whisper away from them. Chuck carried on flying past the other dragon, looping back round to attack it from behind. He swelled a searing hot ball of fire in his mouth and flung it aggressively towards Lucian. The fireball hit the dragon's tail and it yelped in pain. *'I hate attacking other dragons,'* Chuck relayed to Nell, *'it's not in my nature.'*

'I know, Chuck,' Nell responded, 'but we don't have much choice here. Try to aim for that disgusting Lucian instead of the dragon – he's the one who deserves it.' She placed a soothing hand on Chuck's forehead to comfort him and encourage him to keep protecting her kingdom.

The battle raged on for what seemed like hours. Both dragons had taken many hits and, whilst Chuck was not affected by the flames of the other dragon, he knew that the princess would be. He was exhausted from dodging the blasts and being shunted by the other dragon. Nell had been knocked and singed a few times. Her cheek was bloody and her hair slightly burnt on the ends. Chuck and Nell turned to swoop for Lucian once more but did not see the glinting metal dagger he held in his hand. As Chuck forcefully shoved the other dragon and made a lunge for Lucian, the magician thrust the dagger under the sun dragon's scales and along his side. Nell's eyes went wide as she felt the awful pain through her connection to Chuck. "No!" she cried, tears filling her eyes.

'I'm alright, princess, but I can't stay in the air much longer,' Chuck's voice filled her head.

'Just a little longer, Chuck, we can do this' Nell thought back, even more determined that she would put an end to Lucian's revenge. At that moment, the dark red dragon flew full force into Chuck, knocking him sideways. Chuck was falling fast, unable to use his wings to keep his height as he was so exhausted from the fight. 'Chuck? We're falling!' Nell yelped in her head, 'Even if you can't fly, could you glide?' she suggested. On hearing her suggestion, Chuck opened his wings and, as the air caught in their magnificent span, their descent slowed. They floated the rest of the distance to the field and landed somewhat gently.

When he saw Chuck go down, James, who was on the other side of the expanse, galloped over to Nell and Chuck on his borrowed horse to help. "Charming," called Nell, as she saw him approaching, "be careful!" Before he could reply, the earth around him seemed to explode. A huge ball of flame enveloped the prince and the horse. Nell had to raise her arm to shield her eyes from the bright oranges and reds of the fire and the billowing smoke that spilled into the surrounding area. "CHARMING!" screamed Nell, distraught. Tears streamed down her face, partially from the smoke but also from what had just happened in front of her. "Charming?" she called again, "Charming!" The princess shouted until her voice was hoarse but she heard no reply.

As Nell turned to face Lucian, a rage boiled within her, bubbling so much that it spilled over the sides. She had had enough; something had snapped. Swinging her leg over Chuck's back, they both took off again, fuelled by fury. "You disgusting, venomous ANIMAL!" she shrieked, incensed. Her eyes began to glow amber as she funnelled her anger into Chuck's mind too. The pair were completely linked now and moved as one.

"What are you going to do, princess?" taunted Lucian arrogantly, unable to see what was really happening, "Go crying to daddy because the bad man hurt your prince charming?"

'Get him,' she told Chuck. Chuck nodded and began to circle the other dragon and Lucian with gathering speed. "This is getting you nowhere, girl," Lucian continued to provoke, "soon I'll take everyone you love for your defiance!" He started to laugh again, a laugh so filled with poison and hatred that the world seemed to shrivel around him. Still, Chuck did not stop. Whilst he was circling, the sun dragon was building a flame hotter than a thousand suns in his throat until it was ready to burst. "Come on then!" yelled Lucian, mockingly, holding his arms in the air, "Is this all you can do?"

'Now!' Nell thought.

Upon the princess' command, Chuck released a steady flow of sweltering hot flame as he circled around Lucian faster and faster. Within seconds, he had created a spiralling inferno in the sky which was getting larger by the moment. Lucian's eyes grew wide as he saw what was happening and tried to escape the blaze. He kicked the scarlet dragon with his metal boots, causing it to bolt forwards but, as it did, the path was blocked by the twister of fire. With no means of escape, Lucian shouted over the sound of the whipping flames, "This isn't the end, girl. You've lost one, you'll lose them all! *Ceangail sinn còmhla,* we are forever bonded, princess. You're just like me!"

"Oh yeah?" Nell replied, "Not anymore, you worthless, vindictive waste of space." With one final breath of fire from Chuck, the inferno turned into a huge burning ball of flame, engulfing Lucian and the other dragon. The countryside echoed with Lucian's roars of anguish and anger and a magnificent green light burst through the sides of the fireball like lightning as he perished. One of the pillars of green energy struck Nell in the chest and she fell from Chuck into the cloud of smoke. Chuck sped down after her and also disappeared into the haze.

Everything was silent on the field. The fireball still raged in the centre and the green tendrils, which were curling now, cast an eerie glow over the smog filled ground. Not a single soul moved. No sounds could be heard save for the distant cries of the kingdom still trying to save their houses from the earlier flames.

26. Aftermath

As the smoke cleared, the kings and queens of both kingdoms rushed onto the meadow. King Alfred and Queen Minerva of Skyrain dashed over to the spot where James was lying. He was a little bruised and singed but otherwise perfectly fine. As they reached him, the prince sat up and coughed roughly, wincing as the movement made his ribs ache. The royals smothered him in a large embrace of joy and relief when they realised he was alright. Hank sat beside Prince James, a little dazed but unharmed. Completely by chance, the blast from the scarlet dragon had missed the pair and the horse by a few metres and, instead, left a burnt crater behind them. James couldn't help but glance over to where Nell had fallen just a short distance away. The ground was scorched and blackened next to where Chuck the dragon lay motionless. King Robert and Queen Lydia of Sundragon approached the creature tentatively, hoping to see their daughter.

Chuck was curled in a tight ball and, though he was not moving, the royal couple could see the rise and fall of his chest. He was alive but where was the princess? The dragon snorted softly and turned to look at the king and queen. He had sadness in his eyes as he uncurled his body to reveal Princess Nell, lying lifeless in the charred grass. She looked fragile like she might break at the slightest breath of wind and on her chest was a charcoal black burn where she had been struck. Her body was in a bad state with cuts and bruises all over and, of course, her hair looked like she had been pulled through a thorn bush and back again. The queen's breath caught in her throat as she saw her daughter and a sob broke through. She knelt next to the princess finding that she no longer had the strength to stand. "My darling," she wept, "my sweet, sweet Elenore." Lydia buried her face in the tatters of her daughter's dress and King Robert stood next to her, his hand on his wife's shoulder, tears streaming down his cheeks.

"Lydia, my love," he whispered, "I know you're upset – I am too – but we can't leave her here like this."

The queen looked up at her husband, "You're right, Robert. Of course, you're right." She shook her head and stood shakily as though her legs might give way at any moment. The king took her hand and squeezed it tightly in his own.

"Sun dragon," he said, "can you walk?" Chuck heaved himself to his feet, stumbling a few times before managing to stand properly. He padded over to Nell, who was still lying unmoving on the floor. He couldn't hear her thoughts now and feared the worst. King Robert gently lifted the princess onto Chuck's back and placed her so that she would be supported between his wings. The unlikely trio began to walk back slowly towards their castle, not wanting to believe what was right before their eyes.

James lurched forward as he saw what was happening. He had to get to Nell. He pushed past his parents, leaving them sat on the ground confused, and staggered clumsily towards his dragon. "Wait!" he cried, a lump forming in his throat as his voice began to crack, "is she...?" James couldn't finish the question; he wasn't sure he really wanted to know the answer. The tears in her parents' eyes as they turned to him were answer enough. James dropped to the floor holding his head in his hands. She couldn't be. As he fought back the flood of tears which threatened to flow down his face, he whispered to himself, "It should've been me."

27. Unexpected

The next few days passed in a blur. King Robert and Queen Lydia had taken Nell back to the castle and laid her in her bed. They couldn't bring themselves to say goodbye just yet. She looked as though she were sleeping peacefully and, for now, they wanted to believe that's exactly what she was doing. James refused to return to Skyrain, though his parents tried to convince him. He wanted to be near the princess for as long as he could. In the end, his parents went back and he was allowed to stay in the castle of Sundragon. He spent his time with Chuck, who stayed by his side as comfort for them both. The king and queen of Sundragon were too busy to worry about the prince much.

On the morning of the fourth day, a servant was cleaning the princess' bedroom when unexpectedly, Nell slowly opened her eyes. The poor maid screamed, dropped everything from her hands and ran out of the bedroom, slamming the door behind her. "Help!" she yelled, "the princess has come back from the dead!" The girl dashed down the corridor, looking for anyone, *someone* to tell and ran straight into Prince James. They both barrelled over onto the floor with a thump. "Oh!" yelped the prince, "are you alright? You look scared." The maid hurriedly got up, colour flooding her cheeks.

"No – I – well yes. I'm afraid I might be going mad," she said shakily.

"Why would you think that?" James asked, puzzled.

"Well, I was cleaning the princess' room just now and I could've sworn I saw her open her eyes," she replied. James didn't wait to hear another word. He leapt up and sprinted down the landing to Nell's bedroom. He slowed to a gentler pace as he reached the room and carefully opened the door. "Princess?" he whispered, "Are you awake?" Not expecting an answer, he closed the door behind him and made his way over to the ornate chair next to the large, four-poster bed.

"Charming?" Nell croaked, "Is that you?" James' jaw dropped and, in his shock, he missed the chair he was about to sit on and promptly landed on the soft, carpeted floor.

"But – but you were," the prince muttered in a daze.

"I was what?" Nell asked. James shook his head. He couldn't believe this was happening. He recalled the image of her lifeless body being carried from the battlefield just a few days before. How was she even alive?

"You weren't breathing when we brought you back here four days ago. I, I thought you were gone," he admitted. Nell's eyes widened. She hadn't expected that. Had she been unconscious that long? She supposed she ought to explain why she may have seemed at death's door.

"Charming," she started, "you know that beam of green light which hit me? Well, that wasn't just fire. It was magic. I've seemed dead or lifeless because my body has had to completely shut down to recover from that. I don't know how it works exactly, but I'm back now. And look; good as new!" Nell smiled weakly. Tears welled in James' eyes and spilled onto his cheekbones as he saw Nell struggle to sit up in her bed.

"Almost," he smiled.

"Anyway," she interrupted pointedly, "I remember what you called me out in the fields. I never told you my real name – never mind *that* name. There's something you're not telling me, isn't there *Christopher*?" James shifted uncomfortably in his chair. He knew this conversation was long overdue and that he would have to tell her eventually. He had just hoped he would have a little more time before he had to explain himself.

"Ah yes, that," James said, barely above a whisper, "I suppose I've got some explaining to do. It's a long story though,"

"I have time," she insisted.

"Okay," sighed James, "but before I begin, my name really *is* James." He looked over at the princess pleadingly but she was resolute. She needed to know and the prince knew he had to be honest. He took a deep breath and began, "I was born Prince James of Skyrain. My mother and father are Queen Minerva and King Alfred but, when I was still a new-born, I was taken from the castle by a gang of thieves. They stole my cradle for the value of the metal and stones it contained but they didn't expect me to be inside it. When they found me, they were far from the palace, out of the kingdom in fact, and just dumped me in the yard of the closest house they saw. That house was Nanny Sally's cottage. She and her husband took me in and raised me as their own. That's how I came to your castle; how I met you. They called me Christopher and, of course, I never knew any differently."

At this point, James glanced up again at Princess Nell, who was sat open-mouthed against her pillow with her blanket pulled up to her chin in anticipation. He rolled his eyes, "You always were a sucker for a good story."

Nell frowned, "Keep going, Charming."

"Alright, I'm going!" James relented and continued with his own story. "I left the palace when Sally's husband – the man I thought was my father – wanted to train me to take over the family blacksmithing business. That's when I was still writing to you. I missed you every day, Nell." The princess winced as she heard him say her name properly for the first time since he had left. James saw this and apologised with his eyes before carrying on, "After three and a half years of training, the king and queen managed to track me down. They took me away kicking and screaming from the parents I knew and back to the castle of Skyrain.

I never received any of your letters after that. At first, I thought you didn't want to write to me anymore, but I heard your conversation with Firestorm that night in the forest."

"You – you did?" Nell stammered, cheeks flushing.

"Yes, sorry for eavesdropping but I couldn't help it. I knew you were familiar and I wanted to know why. I felt so awful when you said that I was the one who never returned your letters. I realised, then, that Nanny Sally must never have sent them on to me. I've thought of you every day since." James paused as he could feel his face changing colour. He tried to stop himself from blushing too much before he carried on, "From that time, I've been trained as a prince – to fight, to rule, and everything that comes with it. I met Chuck not long after I was taken back to Skyrain and he became my closest friend at a time when we were both in need of someone to trust. And that's it; that's my story."

The prince and princess sat in silence for some time,. Nell tried to process everything that James had told her. James tried to guess how Nell was taking the news. Her expression had become almost impossible to read whilst she was deep in thought. Finally, James couldn't wait any longer and blurted, "Can you ever forgive me, Nell? I didn't want to leave you in the first place. Please, I've almost lost you again twice in the last week. I don't know if I can handle it again." The princess stared at him, unblinking, as he spoke. Her lips were pursed tightly together and her eyebrows were knitted together on her forehead.

A smile twitched at the corner of Nell's mouth, "I can't believe it's really you. I can't really *not* forgive you when you brought me back from – well – whatever that weird spell was. So yes, Kiff, I forgive you." James' mouth broke into a beaming grin and he lunged towards the princess, wrapping her up in a tight hug.

"Oh, Nell, thank you. I don't know what I would've done if you said no. Though I think I prefer Charming now," he laughed, relieved.

"Ow, *ouch*!" Nell flinched as James squeezed her. Immediately, he let go, bringing his hands to her shoulders instead.

"Sorry," he said, "I didn't mean to hurt you." As the prince backed away, Nell's blue eyes were drawn to his warm, golden ones. They gazed at each other without saying another word, both smiling like idiots. Nell couldn't help but notice the way his tousled, sandy hair fell over his eyes now, almost as messy as hers. Slowly, each found themselves leaning towards the other until, finally, they were nose to nose. Nell breathed in sharply as she felt James' breath on her lips. They both closed their eyes in anticipation, about to close the remaining distance between them.

Just then, the door burst open and Nell's parents rushed into the room. The prince and princess quickly pulled apart and looked away from each other, embarrassed. The king and queen didn't even notice what was happening; they were too focused on seeing their daughter. "My little Nell," King Robert cried.

"Oh, my Elenore," Lydia sobbed as she cradled the princess gently, "I'm so glad you're back." James slipped out of the room discretely, leaving Nell and her family to spend some time together. He knew they hadn't really seen her since she first got lost in the forest. They deserved some family time.

The prince left a note for Nell on the table in the entrance hall to the castle. He gathered his things and left for his own kingdom. Now he knew she was alive, it was time for him to see his own parents; he knew they would be waiting. James found his dragon in the stable and called to him, "Come on, Firestorm, time to go home." Chuck looked at him and snorted. "What?" James retorted, "Aren't you coming buddy?" Chuck yawned and snorted again, unimpressed that his best friend wouldn't call him by his real name. "No," James said, "no you can't want me to start calling you *that* can you?" Chuck roared loudly in the prince's face. "Oh, for goodness sakes, fine. Come on then, Chuck, let's go." The dragon leapt up happily and bounded over to James. They took off smiling, soaring into the sky and heading for home.

29. Hank

The next morning, James had just left the large, arched doorway of his castle and headed for the stables to see Chuck and Ilana, when he heard a muffled squeaking sound. He looked down at his satchel, which was slung over his shoulder, and lifted the flap. He gasped as he saw Nell's little pet hawk snuggled up asleep in the corner, cheeping peacefully to himself. James scooped him up into the palms of his hands and said fondly, "What are you doing in there, little guy? Nell will be wondering where you've got to." The small bird peeped through sleepy eyes at James and squeaked happily. Seeing the prince, he woke up properly and fluttered his wings, landing on James' shoulder. "Alright, Hank," James said, "let's go and see Chuck so we can get you home." James, with Hank perched on his shoulder, strode quickly across the large, well-kept gardens. When they got to the stable, Chuck grunted in greeting and his eyes lit up when he saw Hank. Ilana growled and began to purr. As James reached his stall, Chuck started to pad his feet excitedly and snort loudly. "Alright, Chuck, alright!" laughed James, "Are you excited to see Hank by any chance?" The dragon jumped, pushing open the half-door to his stall and ran out into the main stable area. He headbutted James affectionately and licked Hank with a slobbery tongue.

Ilana leapt over her own stable door and joined in the reunion. They all made their way back out into the gardens and Chuck sat down, eagerly waiting for James to get on his back. "Don't you want to know where we're going first?" James asked, amused. Chuck tilted his head to one side, waiting to find out. "Oh, fine, I'll tell you. We're going to see Nell," the prince said. Chuck roared with delight and, once James, Hank and Ilana were ready, the dragon took off gracefully into the skies and headed in the direction of the Kingdom of Sundragon.

Stood at the entrance to the castle of Skyrain, James' parents watched as he flew away on the sun dragon. The king and queen looked at each other thoughtfully. "Minerva, dear," King Alfred said, "do you remember what you said about James and the princess?"

"I do, Alfred, yes. I'm still sure it's true. He's in love with her," she replied wistfully.

"I'm beginning to wonder if it's really such a bad thing, Minerva. Do you think, perhaps, that they might be the ones?" the king asked.

"The ones to what, darling?"

"To bring our kingdoms back together again,"

"Do you know, I think they might," Minerva mused, "they just might." The pair smiled, both lost in their own thoughts, as they watched the silhouette of their son getting smaller and smaller until it was just a speck on the horizon.

30. Forgiveness

The afternoon sun cast a rosy glow on the intricate gardens of Sundragon's castle. On a small bench by an ancient oak tree, Princess Nell was taking a breather from her walk and was staring up at the clear blue sky. In the distance, she could make out what looked like a large bird flying over the forests. The princess inhaled the sweet, fresh garden air and smiled. She had been appreciating the small things much more after her near-death experience and she loved spending as much time outside as she could. Nell was about to stand up when a large gust of wind blew her backwards and she nearly fell over. She raised her hands to shield her eyes from the dirt which was swept up from the floor by the sudden breeze. As she lowered her arm, Nell's eyes widened in surprise at what she saw. There, in front of her, was Prince James grinning like an idiot. "Charming!" she beamed and hurried over to where he was sat astride Chuck. Before she could reach them, she lost her balance and stumbled to the floor. James leapt off the dragon and rushed to her side, catching her before she hit the ground.

"Careful, princess. You need to take it easy," scolded James caringly. Leaning on the prince, Nell managed to pull herself to her feet. They both stood up and ended up closer than either of them expected.
"Oh," breathed Nell. James cupped his hand around the nape of her neck and tangled his fingers in her hair, pulling her closer. Instinctively, Nell closed her eyes, tilting her head upwards. Chuck snorted loudly, unimpressed and Ilana roared disapprovingly. Nell backed away, her cheeks turning a dark shade of crimson

Sighing, James looked at Nell, "I brought someone to see you," he said, trying to break the tension whilst rubbing the back of his head. He turned around and gestured to the bird sat on Chuck's back.

"Hank!" cried Nell, "where have you been? I've missed you!" Hank flapped over to the princess and she cradled him in her arms, kissing his forehead tenderly. "Did you wander off with Charming here?" she giggled. Hank squeaked apologetically. "It's alright, you're back now and you're okay," she whispered and nuzzled the hawk close to her. After a warm reunion, Nell turned to James. "Charming, there's something we need to do," she said seriously.

"Okay," James replied, "what do you need?" Nell moved slowly over to Chuck; Hank was still snuggled in her arms.

"We need to go back to the mountains," she said resolutely. James looked a little shocked but remained silent; he knew she was determined to go and, this time, he would make sure she was safe. James hopped onto Chuck's back and offered Nell a hand as he knew she wouldn't be able to climb up on her own. The princess eyed his hand suspiciously, debating whether to accept his help. She had never needed or wanted it before but this time was different. Looking at James with trust in her eyes, she took his hand and swung herself round onto the dragon's back. Ilana looked up at them from the grass.

"Sorry, Ilana, you'll have to stay here," James smiled.

"Chuck," Nell whispered, "you know where to go." The dragon nodded and took off without another sound.

*

They soared over the fields and forests until they reached the same plateau where Nell and Chuck had been held captive. The sun dragon landed softly and James helped the princess down from his friend's back, wrapping his hands around her waist. They looked around to see the site abandoned. The bonfire was burnt out, the tents had gone but the cages were still full of dragons. They both gasped at the horror of the sight before them. Though they had seen it before, it was no less terrible. "We have to set them free," said Nell sadly, "they can't stay like this."

"You're right, I'll cut the locks on the cages; you and Chuck can sort the chains," James agreed. The prince unsheathed his sword and ran around the plateau, slicing the locks on the cages with his blade. The doors swung open one by one and the dragons started to cry as they anticipated their freedom. Nell and Chuck followed James around the cages. With the princess' guidance, Chuck used his searing hot flames to melt the chains which held the dragons captive. As the dragons became free of their chains, they slowly unfolded their wings and made their way out of the cages. "Wow," Nell breathed, looking up. All the dragons were now free and, all at once, they took off, a mass of flapping wings, and soared into the skies. James came to stand next to the princess.

"Yeah," he agreed, "wow." Only, James wasn't looking at the dragons.

Nell turned away, expecting the dragons to head back to their homes but James hesitated, wanting to see where they went. "Nell, wait a minute," he said, frowning. Nell turned to face him.

"Why?" she asked.

"Look," James gestured to the dragons, who were now flying back down to the plateau and all landed in a tight group before the prince, princess and Chuck.

"What are they doing?" Nell asked, puzzled.

"I was hoping you could tell me," James joked. Nell nodded slowly to the dragons and Chuck did the same. The dragons roared loudly and blasted flames into the air.

"They have forgiven us," Nell stated.

"Wait, what?" James said, surprised.

"They have forgiven us, for what happened to them and their ancestors," Nell repeated. James rubbed the back of his head sheepishly.

"I always forget you can understand them," he grinned, "so they like us now?"

"Pretty much, yes," Nell smiled, "let's go home." James helped the princess onto Chuck's back and hopped on in front of her. She wrapped her hands around his waist and he couldn't help but smile. Hank perched on Chuck's head as he liked to feel involved but couldn't fly as high as the dragon. Chuck began to fly towards the castle of Sundragon to return Nell to her parents. As they glided away from the mountains, the rest of the dragons took flight and followed their path back to the kingdom. They flew across the forests and over the town where people began screaming and running for cover. When they realised that the creatures were not attacking them, they started to peak out of their homes to see what was going on. Finally, the prince and princess, along with their escort of dragons, landed softly in the castle gardens. James lifted Nell off Chuck's back and onto her feet.

The king and queen of Sundragon peered cautiously out of the grand castle entrance. Their eyes fell on Nell. "What's all this, Nell?" King Robert asked, puzzled.

"Where have all these dragons come from?" continued her mother. Nell smiled and looked at James. The prince smiled back and shrugged; he wasn't about to tell the princess what to do.

"Mother, father, come and join us outside," Nell said. Her parents stepped out into the garden, looking at Nell quizzically. Once they were next to James, the princess continued, "The dragons are here to make amends, if you are willing, Papa." The king looked from Nell to the dragons to his wife, shocked. Queen Lydia smiled tenderly at her husband and encouraged him to respond.

"Oh, well I," he stammered, "I never thought I would live to see this. I'm honoured that they want to forgive our people." Nell grinned, "Why don't you tell them yourself? Our family can understand them, Papa!"
"I -wait- we can?" King Robert said. Nell nodded enthusiastically at her father and, taking his hand, slowly led him to the front of the group of dragons.

King Robert cleared his throat and looked at the large number of mythical creatures on his lawn. He swallowed his reservations and spoke to them, "Thank you, all of you. I'm humbled to have your forgiveness for our kingdom." The dragons roared loudly and bowed their heads to the king and queen. "Yes," King Robert replied, "it would be wonderful to have dragons in the kingdom again!" Nell laughed at the look of confusion on her father's face as he realised he had just spoken to and understood a dragon.
"See, Papa, I told you that you could do it!" she said. The king walked back to Queen Lydia and swept her up in an affectionate hug. Nell turned to James and put her hand on the nape of his neck. She kissed him passionately and, after a moment of surprise, the prince returned her kiss. He pulled away momentarily and mumbled, "Finally," before finding the princess' lips again. Hank blushed and hid his face behind his wing, whilst Chuck snorted in their faces. "Okay, okay, Chuck," Nell giggled, "I'll leave him alone." Chuck settled down on the grass, seemingly satisfied.

Nell and James stood side by side, hands intertwined, and looked at the scene before them. They smiled at each other as the dragons took off, one by one, back into the sky to find their families – the ones who managed to evade capture. Their silhouettes were framed on the horizon by the golden and orange hues of the evening sun as it set over the Kingdom of Sundragon.

Epilogue

In the months that followed, things began to change for the two kingdoms. The day after King Robert made peace with the dragons, they returned to make the kingdom their home. People and dragons started to work together to create a better life for all involved and they each got used to their new companions. After intense debate and many arguments and meetings, the kings of the two kingdoms finally found a middle ground and became allies once more. Nell and James really did manage to reunite their families after generations of hatred. The prince and princess made up for lost time and spent almost every waking minute with each other, catching up and getting to know one another properly again. They still enjoyed each other's company as much as when they were younger. Eventually, their friendship did blossom into romance and, much to the delight of their parents and the two kingdoms, they got engaged a few months later. The wedding was to be a grand affair – once Nell had fully recovered.

When the dragons returned from the mountains, they brought many of their families who had managed to evade capture. In amongst them, there was a small family of sun dragons, Chuck's family. After many years, Chuck had finally been reunited with his parents and siblings, who took up residence on the roofs of the castle of Sundragon, just as they had before. Hank became more independent and spent lots of time with Chuck, who helped the hawk become a more confident flier. Ilana spent her days roaming the forests on the outskirts of the kingdom but loved when the prince and princess came to visit her.

So, it's fair to say that, whilst Princess Elenore of Sundragon may not have been a typical fairy tale princess, she certainly got her own version of a fairy tale ending.

And they lived happily ever
after...

...well, almost – life is rarely that perfect!